I FUNNY TV

1 3 5 7 9 10 8 6 4 2

Young Arrow
20 Vauxhall Bridge Road
London SW1V 2SA

Young Arrow is part of the Penguin Random House group of companies
whose addresses can be found at global.penguinrandomhouse.com

Penguin
Random House
UK

First published by Young Arrow in 2016

First published in the United States of America by
Little, Brown and Company in 2015

www.randomhouse.co.uk

A CIP catalogue record for this book
is available from the British Library

Hardback ISBN 9781784753979
Trade paperback ISBN 9781784753986

Printed and bound by Clays Ltd, St Ives Plc

MIX
Paper from
responsible sources
FSC
www.fsc.org   FSC® C018179

Penguin Random House is committed to a sustainable future
for our business, our readers and our planet. This book is
made from Forest Stewardship Council® certified paper.

PART ONE
the End?

Chapter 1

TV OR NOT TV?

Hi, I'm Jamie Grimm, and I really hope you watch my brand-new TV show if I ever actually do one.

See, when I won the Planet's Funniest Kid Comic Contest out in Hollywood, one of the prizes was the chance to star in my own television show on the BNC network.

But I may never really get that chance, because, let's face it, there are so many TV-type things I can't do very well. A cop show is definitely out, because I wouldn't be very good at chasing the bad guys down dark alleys.

Excuse me? Could you guys come back here so I can arrest you? I'd really appreciate it!

I'd be no good on a *Survivor*-type show, either. Especially if it was on a desert island with lots of sand.

Yep, I liked visiting Hollywood, but Long Beach on Long Island is my real home. So, basically, I'm back at the funniest place on earth: middle school.

Luckily, I have some pretty awesome friends. For instance, Jimmy Pierce and Joey Gaynor. They both walk with me to school most mornings.

Well, they walk. I *roll*.

But what's supercool about Gaynor and Pierce is that they never treat me like I'm different or handicapped (I hate that word—it makes me sound like a racehorse). As Gaynor put it once, "You'll just always be shorter than us, dude."

Whenever we come to a major uphill, Gaynor and Pierce don't hurry behind me to push me like I'm an overgrown baby in a stroller. But they might casually grab hold of a handle and give me a gentle assist without ever mentioning it.

Jimmy Pierce, by the way, is a certifiable genius. He's so smart, he once told me that elephants are the only mammals that can't jump. "Elephants and *me*," I reminded him.

Joey Gaynor? He's just certifiable. Lives on the edge of the edge. He has tattoos, nose rings, and those little metal studs that look like steel zits. Recently, he had a metal spike pierced through his ear. Made his lobes look like barbecued shrimp on a skewer.

Every morning on our way to Long Beach Middle School, we pass an elementary school.

When the kids see us coming, they crowd around the edges of the playground and start shouting jokes at me through the chain-link fence. Most of the punch lines are pretty corny, but the kids are cute.

Plus, they're the ones who voted for me when I did the Planet's Funniest Kid Comic finals.

So, of course, we always stop and listen.

Even when it turns out to be a big mistake.

Chapter 2

LAUGHING MY BUTT OFF

We're running a little late, but the kids keep cracking jokes at us.

"One more," I tell them.

"Hey, Jamie?" says this redheaded girl with freckles. "Why do golfers wear two pairs of pants?"

"I don't know. Why?"

"In case they get a hole in one."

Hey, they're fourth and fifth graders telling the same jokes fourth and fifth graders have told since forever. Sometimes I pretend they're so hilarious that I have to let out a big belly laugh and pop a wheelie.

Today, I make a mistake. I do my wheelie-popping a little too close to the curb.

Gaynor and Pierce haul me up and casually slide me back into my chair. This is another reason I love going to school with my wingmen.

Our friend Gilda Gold happens to be coming up the street with her video camera when I do my backflip dive into the gutter. Gilda's always making funny movies. I sometimes star in them—even when I don't know her camera is rolling.

"Hilarious reverse somersault, Jamie," she tells me when I'm back in my seat. "If your head ever gets too big from being a major celebrity, I'll post that backward butt flop on the Internet. Maybe send it to TMZ."

"Thanks," I say with a smile.

Of course, I'm not worried about Gilda posting her video clip online.

Nobody would watch it. I'm not really a celebrity anymore. I'm just a kid who, once upon a time, won a joke-telling contest on TV.

A kid who should know not to pop wheelies too close to the curb. Especially near a puddle.

My soggy underwear stays squishy all day.

Chapter 3

MY BULLY-PROOF VEST

Gilda, Gaynor, Pierce, and I are yukking it up as we head down the hall to our lockers.

All the WELCOME HOME and JAMIE = FUNNY banners have been taken down. There are no more balloons or streamers. There's one congratulations card still stuck to my locker door, but it's barely hanging on to its double-stick tape.

I guess you could call this part of my life *I Just Jamie*.

I mean, what are you supposed to do after your wildest dream comes true? Did I hit my peak in middle school when I won the comedy contest? What if BNC never wants to do a TV show starring a funny kid in a wheelchair? Is it all downhill from here?

If it is, at least I can coast.

Especially if my cousin, Stevie Kosgrov, the school's meanest bully, gives me a shove. Which, incidentally, he does right now.

Oof.

But I'm not really afraid of Stevie anymore, because I've discovered a very powerful secret weapon to defeat him: comedy. A few well-aimed zingers are, in my opinion, one of the best ways to burst a bully's bubble.

So when he threatens to give me a wedgie, I say, "You're really good at giving wedgies, Stevie. Do you practice yanking up your own underwear at home? Is that why you always walk so weirdly?"

As I'm giving Stevie Kosgrov a taste of his own medicine, a new kid lumbers up the hallway. This guy is a giant with more blond hair than the entire cheerleading squad. He sort of shoves Stevie aside and glares down at me.

I had a growth spurt during my growth spurt.

A bunch of other kids' lunches.

"You're Jamie Grimm, right?"

I smile. "What'd you recognize first? My face or my wheelchair?"

"Your big, fat mouth."

O-kay. So much for bonding with the giant who woke up on the wrong side of the beanstalk this morning.

"I'm Lars Johannsen," he says. "My family just moved here from Minnesota."

I think Johannsen (who, by the way, is the *size* of Minnesota) is Scandinavian. I wouldn't be surprised if he were half Viking. The plundering-and-pillaging half.

"I was rooting for Chatty Patty," he says. "Voted for her fifteen times. I punched in her eight-hundred number so hard, I broke my phone."

Quick backstory: Patricia Dombrowski, who calls herself Chatty Patty, is one of the comedians

I defeated out in Hollywood when America cast its votes via telephone and text message, just like they do on *America's Got Talent* and that other show, *America's Got Telephones*.

Patricia Dombrowski lives in Moose Lake, Minnesota. I have a funny feeling this new kid, Lars (which, I'm guessing, is Swedish for *large*), is the moose they named the lake after.

Johannsen bends down so we can go nose to nose and I can smell the pickled herring he ate for breakfast.

"Patty should've beaten you."

I just gulp.

"But that's okay. I'll beat you for her."

"Whoa," says Stevie Kosgrov. "Hold up, newbie. Jamie Grimm is mine."

"Who are you?" Johannsen says to Stevie.

"The name's Kosgrov. Top bully at this school, three years running. If you want to take a shot at the crip, get in line. Behind me."

"Fine. If I'm behind you, it'll be easier to kick your butt."

Two seconds later, Stevie is sprawled out on the floor.

Then it's my turn. One shove and I'm flat on my back, staring up at fluorescent-light fixtures. Again.

Yep. It's just like old times. Only now I have a new bully to worry about.

But guess what? So does Stevie Kosgrov!

Chapter 4

DOWN AT THE DINER

After Lars Johannsen destroys what I thought was my indestructible joke-based Anti-Bully Defense System, I know exactly where I need to go after school: my uncle's diner, Frankie's Good Eats by the Sea.

I need to make sure I've still got it.

It being the ability to make people laugh, not the newest bruise on my butt.

As you can probably tell, Uncle Frankie's diner has been totally rebuilt, refurbished, and remodeled. That's because Good Eats by the Sea became Good Eats *Under* the Sea when Hurricane Sam came ashore a few months back.

Uncle Frankie is, hands down, my favorite relative.

That's why I gave him so much of my prize money. Yep, my one million dollars is basically gone. The government took out a big chunk in taxes right away. Then I helped my other aunt and uncle buy a new house, and I put some money away for college or a future medical miracle. The rest paid for rebuilding the diner.

And Uncle Frankie deserved every penny. After all, he was the first person who thought I might have some kind of comedic talent.

He saw me working behind the counter, where I had fun cracking up his customers with nonstop one-liners. I'd memorized them out of joke books when I was in a hospital, where my doctors truly believed that laughter is the best medicine. It also tastes better than most cough syrups.

Uncle Frankie's also the one who first pointed me in the direction of the Planet's Funniest Kid Comic Contest, and then stood by me for the whole ride, even the bumpy parts. And the scary parts. And the sad parts between the bumpy and scary parts.

More than anybody else, Uncle Frankie helped me put my life back together. I wanted to return the favor.

Now the diner looks great. Very sparkly and shiny. One whole wall is filled with classic yo-yos. Once upon a time, when Uncle Frankie was just a little older than me, he was the yo-yo champ of all of Brooklyn, a place where everybody's first name is Yo. As in: "Yo, Ashley! Yo, Tommy! Yo, Adrienne!"

Uncle Frankie also put in a brand-new, state-of-the-art digital jukebox. It only plays golden oldie doo-wop music, because that's the only music Uncle Frankie likes. "It has a good beat," he says. "You can yo-yo to it."

When I roll into the diner, Uncle Frankie is all smiles.

"Yo, Jamie. How was school?"

"Great," I say, because even though Uncle Frankie is awesome, he's still an adult. And sometimes you just don't want any adult, even your favorite one, to know you're being bullied. Again. "Need any help behind the counter?"

"Does the pope wear a pointy hat?"

I ring up my first customer and, since he had the spaghetti, I try some George Carlin on him.

"If you ate pasta and antipasto, would you still be hungry?"

Blank stare from him. Flop sweat from me.

I try another one-liner on him: "When cheese has its picture taken, what does it say?"

I get zilch.

Finally, I give up.

And *that's* when he recognizes me.

"Oh, right," he says. "You used to be Jamie Grimm. That kid on TV. You used to be funny."

Yep. I *used* to be me.

Chapter 5

CREAKY COMEDY?

Somebody once said, "If you fall off a horse, you need to get back on."

I think it might've been Paul Revere, after he shouted, "The redcoats are coming!" He spooked his horse so badly, it turned into a bucking bronco and tossed him out of the saddle. Anyway, that's what I need to do. Only without the horse.

I need to get back onstage and make some people laugh again.

I have a feeling my comedy muscles have gotten a little soft since the final round of the Planet's Funniest Kid Comic Contest. I haven't been in front of an audience in weeks.

Then, just like Lars Johannsen, it hits me.

I should hold my *own* comedy contest, for

elementary-school kids, like the ones who shout jokes at me every morning.

I could call it Jamie Grimm's Funniest Little Kids in the Whole Wide Universe Competition.

The competition would be open to kids from kindergarten to fifth grade. That way I wouldn't be showcasing the same bunch of comics who were in my bracket. We could do the show at the diner. Uncle Frankie could clear out a space in the main room, rig up a microphone, maybe rent a spotlight. I would be the master of ceremonies, rolling out between comics to entertain the crowd.

It would give me something to work for. I'd need all-new material, because everybody's already seen most of my old stuff on TV. Uncle Frankie could give the winner a lifetime supply of chili fries. The local newspaper could put their picture in the paper. The winner, not the chili fries.

I head home to Smileyville to bounce this brainstorm off my uncle and aunt Smiley.

I call the Kosgrovs' house "Smileyville" because they (and their dog) never look like they're having a very good time.

Happy HOLIDAYS

from the KOSGROV Family
SERIOUSLY, THIS IS US LOOKING HAPPY!

I've had better luck making lawn gnomes laugh. But, all in all, the Smileys have been extremely good to me. They took me in when I got out of the hospital and did everything they could to make their home wheelchair accessible.

They became my new family right after I'd lost my old one.

They also gave me Stevie for a housemate, but, hey, nobody's perfect.

Smileyville has moved a little closer to the shore because I used some of my prize money to help make the down payment on a bigger, nicer house after their old one got wrecked by Hurricane Sam. The Smileys, of course, are still the Smileys. They just have more room to frown in.

And I still live in the garage. Only now it's a two-car garage. What can I say? I love rolling up my bedroom doors with a flick of the remote control.

I also love my new roommate.

It's Uncle Frankie's classic 1967 Ford Mustang convertible, parked right next to my bed. It's here because the car will be mine the minute I turn sixteen and get my driver's license. We're going to outfit it with hand controls for the brakes and gas pedal—and then I can hit the highway.

I'll be able to go wherever I want to go.

I like seeing Uncle Frankie's cherry-red Mustang every night right before I fall asleep.

Sometimes, I even dream about my new set of wheels.

And all the freedom they'll bring me.

Chapter 6

DOWN IN FROWN TOWN

That night, over dinner, the Smileys react to my new comedy contest idea the same way they react to everything.

Yep. They're frowning. Except Ol' Smiler, the dog. He's groaning and covering his eyes with his paws.

"You've already won one contest," says my aunt, Mrs. Smiley. "Why do you need another trophy?"

"I wouldn't be competing," I try to explain. "I'd just be the host. This is for all the kids in elementary school who want to be comedians."

"Why?" asks Mr. Smiley.

"Huh?"

"Why would these kids want to be comedians? You already won all the prize money. Do they get a chance to star in their own TV show, too?"

I decide to let the subject drop.

The dinner table is already tense enough.
Stevie's hand is shaking so badly, peas are bouncing
off his spoon like Mexican jumping beans.

"Are you all right, Stephen?" asks Mr. Smiley.

"Fine," he squeaks.

"How was school?" asks his mom.

"Fine." His voice is so high-pitched, it makes Ol' Smiler yelp.

"Well, son," says Stevie's father, "you know what they say about eighth grade: The third time's the charm."

And then, when everybody is concentrating on chewing Mrs. Smiley's meat loaf (it's like gnawing on a steel-toed work boot), Stevie glares at me. *This is all your fault!* he silently mouths.

Sorry, I mouth back. *But now you know how it feels to be bullied.*

"Mommy?" says Mary, Stevie's little sister. "Stevie and Jamie are talking with their mouths full of food, but no words are coming out."

"I'm working on my ventriloquist act," I joke. And then the kicker slips out before I can stop it: "Stevie's going to be my dummy."

I hunch my shoulders up to my ears, bracing for the punch I know Stevie should be throwing my way as payment for that crack.

But he doesn't budge. His spoon hand just

trembles some more. Pinging peas dance across his plate like popcorn in the popper. Ol' Smiler quickly vacuums up the ones that fall on the floor. At least *someone's* happy.

"Stevie?" says Mrs. Smiley. "Why are you so shaky? Did you eat candy bars for lunch again?"

"I'm fine. May I please be excused from the table?"

Wow. Stevie has never, *ever* asked to be excused from the table. Usually, he sits there until everybody else is gone so he can lick their plates clean.

Thinking about Lars Johannsen intimidating Stevie, I'm reminded of a corny joke:

What do you call a kid who's being threatened by the meanest bully in school?

An ambulance.

Chapter 7

RETURN OF THE LIVING DEAD

The next morning, I head off to school, eager to share my kids' comedy contest idea with Pierce, Gaynor, and especially Gilda.

But I have to be careful. Zombies shuffle down the sidewalks of Long Beach every morning.

They lurch along, dragging their feet. These guys are dropping body parts all over the place.

"Hey, kid!" one of the zombies groans at me. "Did you hear about the zombie who was expelled from school?"

"Um, no. What'd he do wrong?"

"He kept buttering up his teacher!"

Do the undead really swarm the streets outside Smileyville?

Well, that's what *I* see, in my imagination.

Mostly, the people I roll past are just sleepy-eyed commuters dragging their feet as they trudge off to work. They usually come back to life after a second cup of coffee and a doughnut. First thing in the morning, I guess they're just dead tired.

I cruise up to the middle school and I'm struck with a couple of surprises:

First, Stevie Kosgrov isn't in the parking lot, shaking down kids for their lunch money.

Second, Uncle Frankie *is* there, waiting for me.

Uncle Frankie looks extremely serious.

It's funny how, sometimes, this whole comedy thing will do that to people.

Chapter 8

HOLLYWOOD CALLING. AGAIN.

I just got off the phone with the bigwigs at BNC-TV," Uncle Frankie tells me. "Remember that producer, Joe Amodio?"

"Sure," I say. "He was the brains behind the whole kid-comedian show."

You should see the pen I used to sign this thing.

BNC INC

PAY TO JAMIE GRIMM   1,000,000~

One Million Dollars (Seriously) DOLLARS

Moolah for Ha-Ha
Money for funny.

Joe Amodio

"Well," says Uncle Frankie, "Mr. Amodio is flying in from Hollywood. He says he wants to talk to you about the prize. Today."

Uncle Frankie is, more or less, my business manager these days. He handles whatever show-business stuff bubbles up so I can concentrate on my schoolwork.

"Uh-oh. Do they want their million dollars back?" I ask. "Because we spent a lot of it…"

Uncle Frankie shakes his head. "Mr. Amodio wants to talk to you about the *other* prize—starring in your own sitcom. Remember?"

Wow! To be honest, I was starting to think that the "chance" to star in my own television pilot for the BNC network was like the Free Parking space on a Monopoly board. I might never land on it.

A *pilot* is what people in Hollywood call the first episode of a TV show. If the pilot is a big hit, then the network might want a whole season of the show. That means you'd need to film about twenty-two more episodes. You'd also need a bigger piggy bank to put all your money.

"But we haven't heard from Mr. Amodio in weeks," I say. "I thought he'd forgotten about me."

Uncle Frankie grins. "Forget about Jamie Grimm? Not possible, kiddo."

I hear a *THUMP-THUMP-THUMP* overhead. Uncle Frankie and I both look up at the sky.

A ginormous BNC news chopper is hovering over Long Beach Middle School.

It kicks up a swirl of dust and clumps of grass as it lands on the recently mowed baseball field.

Like my helicopter, Jamie? It's a flying clown car.

Joe Amodio comes bounding over to shake my hand.

"There he is," he says as he pumps my hand. "Funniest kid on the planet. Thanks for taking this meeting, Jamie baby."

This is a meeting?

In a school parking lot?

Where's everybody else going to sit?

Chapter 9

FUNNY BUSINESS AS USUAL

Allow me to make a few introductions," says Mr. Amodio as all the Hollywood types cluster around me and Uncle Frankie. "This is Brad Grody, our director."

Up steps a hipster guy with a long beard. He's dressed in work boots, jeans, a plaid flannel shirt, nerd glasses, and a thick headband. I guess when he's not directing TV shows, he's a nearsighted lumberjack.

> Let me make one thing clear, kid— I am NOT the guy from the paper towel rolls.

"Full disclosure," the director tells me. "I voted for Chatty Patty in the comedy contest. Totes awk. Whatevs. But, YOLO, am I right?"

I have no idea what he's talking about.

"And this funmeister," says Mr. Amodio, pointing to a skinny guy in even thicker glasses, "is Stewart Johnson. Best gag writer in all of Hollywood."

"Hiya, kid. As the bacon said to the tomato, 'Lettuce work together.' This your school?" "Yes, sir."

"Hey, speaking of school, do you know why math books are so sad?"

> What do you do if a teacher rolls her eyes at you? Pick them up and roll 'em right back.

"No. I never really—"

"They've got nothing but problems! Yeah, I can't even count how many times I've failed math."

"He's hysterical," says Mr. Amodio. "Am I right?"

"Well…"

"After months of brainstorming," he continues, "we've come up with the Big Idea for your sitcom, Jamie. We're calling it…"

He makes a frame with his hands like he's reading a billboard. I half-expect to hear a trumpet fanfare.

"Are you ready? *Jamie Funnie.* We spell *funny*

with an *ie*, just like your name. You, Jamie, play the title character, who's also named Jamie. Because, face it, kid—any way you spell it, you funny!"

"And if you're not," adds Johnson, the writer, "we'll make everyone think you are by writing you some new gags."

Great. Because so far, that's what all this guy's jokes make me want to do.

Gag.

Chapter 10

HOLLYWOOD INVADES
MY MIDDLE SCHOOL

Mr. Amodio and the Hollywood types march into school and basically take over the faculty lounge, a room I've always wanted to see, by the way.

Did you know the teachers have their own soda machine and a refrigerator? There's also a coffeepot that smells like wet-gym-sock soup. On the plus side, someone brought in a chocolate cake.

Suddenly, I want to become a teacher!

"We were just having some cake," Mrs. Kanai, one of my favorite teachers, says to the gaggle of Hollywood geese. "It's Mrs. Kressin's birthday."

"She's in charge of our drama club," I say. Then I tell Mrs. Kressin, "These guys are from Hollywood.

They're thinking about putting me in a TV show."

"Oh, my," says Mrs. Kressin, sounding kind of giddy. "That certainly is exciting. Every young performer's dream come true! Are you currently casting any supporting roles?"

"Yeah," says Joe Amodio as he shows Mrs. Kressin the door. "We might need a few teachers. But only if they know how to take direction."

"Certainly," flutters Mrs. Kressin. "What is my direction for this scene?"

"Exit stage right," says Brad Grody. "Immediately."

The teachers take away their cake while the suits fill the table with briefcases, laptops, and file folders.

"Please," says Joe Amodio, "everyone, grab a seat."

"Except Jamie," cracks Stewart the joke machine. "He brought his own!"

Everybody laughs. But while they're laughing, they're watching me to see if I'm going to laugh, too.

I give them a tiny "ha-ha" because I don't want to be rude.

They take the hint and immediately stop chuckling.

"Jamie," says a very tall lady. *Her* nerd glasses

have purple frames. "I'm Rose Skye Wilder, executive producer on the show. Let me put this out on the stoop and see if the cat licks it up."

"Huh?" I say.

"Let's put it on a train and see if it reaches Milwaukee."

"Whaa?"

"She's going to run something up the flagpole and see if you salute," says Uncle Frankie. "Right?"

"Exactly."

I'm still confused.

"She's going to tell you their idea for the sitcom pilot and see if you like it," Uncle Frankie explains. Then he leans back in his chair a little. "I've been in show business a little longer than Jamie. I'm more familiar with the lingo."

Ms. Wilder lays out the basic premise behind *Jamie Funnie*.

"It's fresh. It's out there. It's never been done before. Jamie Grimm will star as Jamie Grimm in a show about Jamie Grimm's daily life and how it feeds him material for his comedy routines."

It's true. My life is a comedic gold mine. Hey, it's middle school.

"At the beginning and end of each episode," she explains, "we'll see Jamie onstage in a comedy club doing jokes based on what's going to happen in that night's episode. He goes up against the school bully, he does jokes about bullies. He eats oatmeal, he does jokes about oatmeal. He buys a pack of bubble gum, we pack in the bubble-gum jokes. So, what do you think, Jamie? It's boffo, am I right?"

Oh, boy.

Rose Skye Wilder seems like a nice lady. I don't want to burst her bubble-gum bubble. But I've studied all the great comics. Practically memorized their TV shows.

"Um," I finally say, "isn't this 'never been done before' show a lot like *Seinfeld*, Jerry Seinfeld's old sitcom?"

"No way," says Joe Amodio.

"Seinfeld was fifteen, twenty years older than you," adds Brad Grody.

"His first name was Jerry, not Jamie," says another one of the suits.

"And," says Ms. Wilder, "*Seinfeld* didn't have an Uncle Frankie or a kid in a wheelchair."

I nod.

They're right.

It's one hundred percent completely different.

Except for where it's not.

Chapter 11

SIGN ON THE DOTTED LINE

We'd shoot on a soundstage here in New York,"
Ms. Wilder continues. "Keep you close to your
friends and family."

"We'd like that," says Uncle Frankie. "Jamie has
a lot of fans at my diner."

"A diner that, by the way, will pick up oodles
of free publicity from the show," says Joe Amodio.
"Because it will be one of our main sets."

Uncle Frankie is thrilled. "Fantastic! If you want,
I can teach you how to flip a burger backward.
People love it. Unless, you know, I miss."

"Terrific, Frankie baby. But before we can flip
burgers behind our backs or do anything else, we
need to know that Jamie is officially on board."

All of a sudden, it sounds like we're going to film
my sitcom on a boat.

Mr. Amodio stands up and holds out his hand. One of the suits sitting next to him pops open her briefcase, pulls out a thick legal document, and slaps it into his open palm.

"What's that?" asks Uncle Frankie.

"Jamie's new contract. It's for the pilot. Just one episode. But if that single episode is the hit I know it will be, we'll be back with an even thicker contract. For twenty-two more episodes and twenty-two times more money."

The suit sitting closest to me opens his briefcase and hands me a very nice pen. The gold kind you'd get as a gift when you graduate from college.

"You can keep it *after* you sign," Suit Man says

when he sees me admiring the shiny pen. I'm used to Bics.

Joe Amodio slides the very important-looking stack of paper across the table to me.

"We just need you to sign everywhere you see the little stickies that say *sign*," says the lawyer, twisting the sparkling pen to life.

"Unfortunately," says Brad Grody, glancing at his very sparkly watch, "I have another meeting in New York City. I'd like to get there…sometime today."

In other words, he wants me to hurry up and sign the contract.

But, for some reason, I can't. My hand is frozen.

Yep. I'm choking again.

Chapter 12

CHOKING ON THE DOTTED LINE

I just sit there, staring at the contract.

I'm squeezing the lawyer's fancy pen so hard, my knuckles turn pinkish white. They sort of look like boiled shrimp.

"Take your time, Jamie," says Joe Amodio. "But I only have the helicopter till noon. Then it has to go do traffic reports."

I nod. And stare. And choke some more.

Do I really want to do this?

Do I want to take my life and turn it into a half hour's worth of lame jokes every week?

What if they want me to say or do things I don't want to say or do?

What if they want to do a sappy show about how I ended up in my wheelchair, which is something I don't want to talk about on national TV?

"Well, Jamie?" says Mr. Amodio, snapping me out of my thoughts.

"We're ready and raring to go," adds Ms. Wilder.

"Just need you to sign on the dotted line," says the lawyer who handed me the pen. He has another pen (this one's silver) up and ready to go, just in case I don't like the gold one clutched in my hand.

"Um," I say, "if it's okay with you guys, I'd like to think this over."

"Think?" says Joe Amodio. "We're from Holly-wood. We don't do that."

"Well," says Uncle Frankie, pushing the stack of papers back across the table toward Mr. Amodio, "here in Long Beach, we don't rush into anything, except the Atlantic Ocean on Super Bowl Sunday."

That makes me smile. Uncle Frankie is a member of the Long Beach Polar Bear Club. Every year, they go for a frigid swim to raise money for the Make-A-Wish Foundation.

We're going in as polar bears and coming out as Popsicles!

Joe Amodio sits down. Snaps his fingers.

Another lawyerly looking guy pops open another briefcase. He hands Mr. Amodio another stack of papers.

"I didn't want to bring this up," says the producer. "But, well, you sort of forced my hand."

"Bring what up?" says Uncle Frankie.

"The fine print." Joe Amodio taps several paragraphs thick with tiny type, the kind you agree to every time you download a new version of iTunes. "You signed this when you won the million dollars out in Hollywood, remember, Jamie?"

I nod. Nervously. "I thought it was like a receipt."

Mr. Amodio grins. Shakes his head. "It was a contract."

"Legal and binding," adds the lawyer. "In all fifty states, Puerto Rico, and Guam."

"What kind of contract?" asks Uncle Frankie.

"For this TV show. That million-dollar prize wasn't really a 'prize.' It was an advance."

"An advance?" I say. "What does that mean?"

"It means, Mr. Grimm," says the lawyer, "that Mr. Amodio has already paid you, in advance, to perform in this pilot."

I gulp.

Because I've already spent a lot of Mr. Amodio's money.

On Smileyville 2 and Uncle Frankie's diner.

If I have to give Mr. Amodio his money back, we might all have to live in Uncle Frankie's van. That wouldn't be much fun. We'd have to cook dinner over the heat vents.

And...I'd have to sleep next to Stevie.

It's not much of a choice.

Chapter 13

ANYBODY GOT A MILLION BUCKS I CAN BORROW?

So, if *that* was a contract," demands Uncle Frankie, "why do you need Jamie to sign this contract, too?"

Joe Amodio shrugs. "Lawyers. What can I say? They love contracts."

"This one specifically covers Jamie's appearance in the pilot," explains one of the guys in a suit.

Whatever it covers, I don't sign it.

Uncle Frankie won't let me.

"Jamie's going to mull it over," he tells Joe Amodio.

"What's there to mull?" says Amodio. "Either Jamie Grimm stars in *Jamie Funnie,* or he has to give me back my one million dollars."

"Plus interest," says the lawyer. "Paragraph fourteen. Subsection D."

"What about the taxes they took out?" asks Uncle Frankie.

"Maybe if you ask nice," says another lawyer, "the government will give you a refund."

I'm shaking my head. "I think they already bought a battleship with my money. Maybe an aircraft carrier."

"Jamie?" says Uncle Frankie, motioning for me to join him over by the door. "Why don't you go to class? Me and Mr. Amodio need to talk some more."

"B-b-but…"

"Listen, kiddo. I don't want you doing anything you don't want to do."

"But the diner…"

"If I have to sell it, I'll sell it. I'll cook burgers out of the back of my van."

"You can't. We'll be sleeping inside."

"Come again?"

"Never mind. I just can't let you lose your diner again, Uncle Frankie."

"And I can't let you do something that makes you miserable," he whispers.

Then he does this thing he does sometimes. He places his hand on my shoulder. It always makes me feel better.

"You ask me, you've already had enough misery for a kid your age," he tells me. "So don't worry, kiddo. We grown-ups are gonna have a little chat. All about bad publicity and you talking about these fine-print shenanigans with your friends at *People* magazine and *Entertainment Tonight*."

Uncle Frankie cracks his knuckles, the way he does when he's loosening up his fingers for a yo-yo demonstration.

"Okay, boys and girls," he says to the Hollywood people. "Let's talk turkey…"

I roll out of the faculty lounge wondering if turkey is the language they speak in Turkey. Or if talking turkey is just something you should only do around Thanksgiving.

The jokes aren't making me feel much better.

If I don't do the show, Uncle Frankie is going to lose his diner. The Smileys might lose their house. My college fund will be back to zero, and if there are any medical treatments that would help me walk again, I wouldn't be able to afford them.

If I do the show, it might end up being really terrible in the hands of those Hollywood people. It could be the death of my comedy career just when I'm getting started. Most of all, I'd lose any hope of ever being a normal kid.

I mull it over.

Then I mull it over again.

In fact, I mull for so long, by the time lunch period rolls around, my stomach is growling. Now *it's* talking turkey.

Enough with the mulling! We're starving down here. Turkey would be nice. Maybe on a roll, with mustard. With a side of pizza... on a burger...

When the bell rings, I head down to the cafeteria, where it's chicken nuggets, buttered noodles, and peas day. By the way, I think schools are the only places in America that actually have buttered noodles on the menu.

I glance over at Stevie Kosgrov, who's sitting all by himself. Peas are bouncing out of his spoon again. He really needs to learn how to spear them with his fork.

"You shaking in your boots like your cousin, Crip?"

Uh-oh. It's Lars Johannsen.

What are you doing out here, Grimm? Shouldn't you be between two slices of bread like the other piles of baloney?

He has six cartons of chocolate milk on his tray. There must be a bunch of sixth graders eating lunch without the aid of a refreshing beverage today.

"I wish I could shake in my boots," I tell Lars. "That would mean my legs were working again."

"You have a smart mouth."

"I guess. Too bad *you'll* never know what it feels like to have an intelligent body part."

"My fist doesn't need to be smart," he says, cocking it back. "It just needs to hurt."

"Mr. Johannsen?"

Finally.

Mr. McCarthy, aka Mr. Sour Patch, comes over. He's the vice principal at Long Beach Middle School and loves disciplining kids so much that he volunteers for lunch duty. Every day. It's sort of his hobby.

Move along, Mr. Johannsen.

Or what, old man?

Or you'll need a tutor in Advanced Algebra to calculate the amount of detention I'll give you.

Finally, Johannsen shuffles away.

I join Pierce, Gaynor, and Gilda at our regular table.

"Where've you been?" asks Gilda. "I was looking everywhere for you."

I don't want to tell her (or anybody else) about my million-dollar dilemma. So I give a very vague reply: "I had this thing. With Uncle Frankie."

"I had a thing once," says Gaynor. "It was in between my toes."

"Was it a fungus?" asks Pierce. "Because I had a fungus thing once."

"This wasn't a fungus thing," I say loudly. I turn to Gilda. "So, why were you looking for me?"

Gilda's eyes brighten the way they always do before she unleashes another brainstorm.

Stand back. This could get intense.

With Gilda, it usually does.

Chapter 1✗

LIGHTS! CAMERA! GILDA!

This is so fantabulous!" Gilda gushes.

"What's up?" I ask.

"I saw this on the Internet. Printed it out."

She hands me a piece of paper she's folded and unfolded like a jillion times. Maybe she's taking up origami.

YOUNG FILMMAKERS:
We're Looking for the FUNNIEST Shorts on the Planet!
ENTER NOW

"It's a kids' funny shorts contest," says Gilda.

"You mean like boxer shorts?" I ask. "The ones with funny stuff printed all over them like rubber duckies or Homer Simpson's face?"

Now everybody at the table is silently staring at me.

"Yo, Jamie," says Gaynor. "You have Homer Simpson underwear?"

"No, I just—"

"This is nothing like that," says Gilda, thankfully cutting me off and moving on. "*Short* means a short film. For this contest, my finished movie has to be between twelve and fifteen minutes long. The winner gets a summer internship at UCLA film school, plus a shot at a full-ride scholarship."

"That's incredible," I say.

"I know." Gilda is beaming. "What the Planet's Funniest Kid Comic Contest did for you, this contest could do for me. Minus, of course, the million dollars."

Right, I think. Of course, I didn't actually win a million bucks, either. It was an "advance," which might soon become a "retreat." But Gilda and the guys don't need to know about that....

"Hey," I say, "a full-ride scholarship is a pretty awesome prize."

"And UCLA is my dream school! Tons of famous movie directors went there for college!"

"Cool."

"And you're going to be my star, Jamie. Gaynor and Pierce will be my crew."

"I'm on camera," says Pierce.

"I'm on lights," says Gaynor. "And bongos. If, you know, there are any bongos in the flick."

I need to stall a little. I might not be able to star in Gilda's movie if I decide to say yes to the TV pilot, which I might need to do to save Uncle Frankie's diner and Smileyville 2. But it doesn't feel right to disappoint a girl you once kissed. More on that later.

Wow. Life sure was easier back in the good old days. (That would be this morning.)

"So, uh, what's the movie going to be about?" I ask Gilda.

"Not sure yet. I'm bouncing a bunch of ideas around. But Vincent O'Neil volunteered to write jokes for you." Hoo-boy. Vincent O'Neil spends most of his time cracking stale jokes and telling everybody he's a million times funnier than me.

But even with corny Vincent O'Neil jokes, if the
million dollars wasn't an issue, I'd rather star in
Gilda's fifteen-minute film instead of my own BNC
sitcom pilot.

Why?

Well, can I let you guys in on a little secret?

Can I be totally honest with you?

I'm nervous. Maybe I *am* shaking in my boots like Lars Johannsen said, even though I don't wear boots. They make my feet sweat.

What if I do the TV pilot and it flops?

What if *Jamie Funnie* is totally *Unfunnie*?

What if I bomb?

My comedy career would be over. Forever. I probably couldn't even get a gig at the grand opening of a gas station.

That's the number one problem with show business. Every chance to hit the big time is also a chance to flop. When you reach for the stars, sometimes you fall out of your chair and wind up flat on your face.

And I don't really want a broken nose to go along with my busted legs.

Chapter 15

SMILEYVILLE TURNS INTO TINSELTOWN

After school, I head home, where the Smileys are buzzing about the possibility of a *Jamie Funnie* TV sitcom.

It turns out that after their meeting with Uncle Frankie ended, the Hollywood crew came to Smileyville and made some pretty hefty promises. I guess they want *everybody* in what's left of my family pressuring me to sign that contract.

"Meryl Streep is going to play me," says Mrs. Smiley, putting her hands over her heart. "I wonder what kind of accent she'll use."

Mr. Smiley struts into the kitchen and, believe it or not, he's smiling.

"I'm Brad Pitt," he says. "And the director wants me to give Brad tips on what it's like to be me. So I've started taking notes. Did you know I brush my teeth with my left hand?"

According to the BNC-TV casting director, a couple of child stars from the Disney Channel are eager to play the younger Smiley kids. And Stevie?

"They're in negotiations with Dwayne Johnson," gushes Mrs. Smiley.

I don't believe it. "The Rock?"

She nods eagerly.

"No way is The Rock playing Stevie," I say. "He's too old."

"Not if they use makeup," says Mr. Smiley.

"And green screens," adds Mrs. Smiley. "That's how they do all sorts of special effects. Green screens and camera tricks and makeup."

I nod very slowly. "Really. Who told you that?"

"Brad Grody. The director on the project. He says that's how they made Yoda look like an old man in the *Star Wars* movies even though he was really played by a very talented toddler."

"Yoda was a puppet," I say.

Mrs. Smiley shakes her head. "Not according to the folks from Hollywood. And I'm sorry, Jamie, but I think they know a little bit more about movie magic than you do."

That night, I'm in my garage bedroom when Stevie actually knocks on the door instead of just barging in.

"I need a favor," he says, sort of timidly.

I arch an eyebrow. Stevie has never asked me for a favor before. And he's never been timid in his whole life.

"Um, what do you want?" I ask.

"When The Rock gets here to play me in the TV show, can he, like, be my bodyguard, too?"

"What?"

"He has all those muscles. I need to borrow a few. To scare off Lars Johannsen."

"Stevie, you don't need The Rock. If a bully is bothering you, just ignore him."

"Well, how do you do that? How do you ignore a moose of a kid who follows you all around town and dumps a sixty-four-ounce Big Slurp in your lap? And what about when he sticks your head down a toilet and flushes it? How do you ignore that?"

I don't say anything.

"Come on, tell me. What's your secret? How do you ignore a bully when he's picking on you?"

I still don't answer.

Because, yep, I'm ignoring him.

Chapter 16

TAKE A WALK (OR ROLL) ON THE BOARDWALK

Later that night, I roll out of the garage and head down to the boardwalk.

The boardwalk is an excellent place to just sit and think. With the stars up above and the surf pounding against the shore, you can be all alone with your thoughts.

Unless, of course, someone is already sitting on your favorite bench.

Which tonight someone is. Not that I actually sit on the bench. I just like to park next to it. The streetlamp lighting is very moody. And the moths dive-bombing into the bright white bulb can be extremely entertaining.

As I roll closer, I realize that the shadowy bench sitter is one of my favorite people, Cool Girl.

Well, that's what I call her, because she's just always so supercool. Nothing fazes her. Also, she has no filter. She always tells the truth, even if you'd rather hear a nice fluffy lie.

Cool Girl's real name is Suzie Orolvsky. In the country where her ancestors lived, they had a severe vowel shortage one winter and everybody fled to America.

By the way, remember how I told you I kissed Gilda once? Well, I've kissed Cool Girl, too. And once, she kissed *me*. Yes, I keep a scorecard.

The main reason I like her so much? Cool Girl

is the one person who I never, ever have to make laugh. She likes it when I'm just me instead of Jamie the Joker.

"Hiya, Jamie," she says when I roll up beside her.

"Uh, hi," I sort of stammer. "Didn't expect to bump into you out here."

"Ditto" is all she says.

Then neither one of us says anything else for a while. We just sit and listen to the soothing sounds of the ocean.

"So," Cool Girl finally says, "trying to make a tough decision?"

"How'd you know?"

She shrugs. "You have a certain grim look, Jamie."

I smile. It's a decent pun. "You must hang out here at night all the time."

"Not really. Not in the winter."

"Speaking of winter..."

"Jamie? No jokes. You can't make the tough choices if you're always hiding behind your next punch line."

So I don't tell her the number one problem with snowshoes. (They always melt.)

"Okay," I say, "here's what's going on. My wildest dream is about to come true. I have a chance to star in my very own TV sitcom."

If I say no, I have to give back the million dollars we used to rebuild my uncle's diner. If I say yes... what if I stink?!
What if my whole life is basically over and done with?
What if this kid comic contest was as far as I was meant to go?
If you only ever win one thing... does that make you a LOSER?!
If I'm not the funniest kid... who am I?
If they're not laughing at my jokes... are they really laughing at me?
What if I'm not supposed to accomplish anything else incredible for the rest of my LIFE?!
What if a seagull poops on my sneakers? Sure, my shoes are white so nobody will see the bird poop, but I'll always know the truth.

"You know, Jamie," says Cool Girl when I finish, "I've never been all that impressed by what you've done or what you've accomplished."

"Really?"

"Nope. What impresses me is who you are: a sweet kid with a huge heart who's always trying to brighten everybody else's day. Like what you did to help out your uncle after the hurricane trashed his diner. You gave him all that money. Who cares if it wasn't really yours to give? It was still totally amazing."

"Thanks," I say.

We sit quietly for a few more minutes.

I break the silence.

"So, um, are we going to kiss again?"

"Don't think so."

"Yeah. Me neither."

Chapter 17

WHO WANTED TO BE A MILLIONAIRE?

The next day, I'm still mulling things over on my way to school.

Do I say yes to the TV show to save Uncle Frankie's diner? If I do, I run the risk of it being a flop and killing my comedy career.

Or do I say no to Joe Amodio and remain a semi-anonymous nobody who, once upon a time, used to be a somebody? At least I'd get to be a normal kid—which, frankly, is all I've really wanted ever since I wound up in this chair.

The second I hit homeroom, Vincent O'Neil starts pitching me "fresh material" for Gilda's short film.

"Big concept," he says, framing the air the way

Joe Amodio did. "Bring back snappy patter. You're an old-fashioned vaudeville comedian. You wear a funny hat. A mustache. Maybe you walk with a cane."

"Um, I don't walk."

"Right. Forget the cane. Forget the walking. We'll get you a small dog instead."

"For what?"

"I don't know. Charlie Chaplin sometimes had dogs in his movies."

"So this is going to be a silent movie?"

"What?" says Vincent. "If it's silent, how can anyone hear the snappy patter?"

"But Charlie Chaplin—"

"Forget Chaplin. Forget the dog."

"Already forgotten."

"You, Jamie Grimm, are the new Gru!"

"From *Despicable Me*?"

"Right."

"We can't do that," I say. "It's already a movie. We'd end up in joke-thief jail."

This is it. The final straw. The one that broke the camel's back when he ordered a milk shake. I'm going to say no to everybody.

To Gilda.

To the TV pilot.

To the elementary-school kids, who don't even know about my idea for a local comedy contest.

But then Gilda Gold comes into the room.

81

I have never seen her look so happy.

"You guys," she says, "I just heard from the Funniest Kids' Shorts on the Planet people. They are sooooo impressed that I know you!"

"Really?" says Vincent.

"Not you. *Jamie*. They told me your big news!"

Uh-oh.

"They did?"

"How come you didn't tell us you were going to star in your own sitcom called *Jamie Funnie?*"

"Well…"

"Doesn't matter. They're super amazed that the star of his own network sitcom pilot has also agreed to star in my short film! They said that with Jamie Grimm playing the lead, I can skip the preliminary screening process and send my video straight to the final judges!"

I'm smiling on the outside. Sweating on the inside. Actually, I'm sweating a little on the outside, too.

"So when do you start shooting the BNC pilot?" Gilda asks eagerly.

"Soon."

So now I have a chance to save Uncle Frankie and the Smileys and to help Gilda.

Even Cool Girl says she likes me best when I do
nice stuff for other people.

I don't think I have a choice here. I take a
deep breath and pull the BNC contract out of my
backpack and sign it.

Even though the only pen I can find is a chewed-
up old Bic.

Chapter 18

SIGNED, SEALED, DELIVERED

During lunch, Mr. Amodio parks his helicopter on the middle-school ball field again to pick up my signed contract.

"Sorry we had to play hardball with you, Jamie baby," he says. "But that's showbiz."

We shake hands. Then I pose for a bunch of selfies in front of the helicopter with my friends while Mr. Amodio does a quick interview with a crew from Channel 6. I think they're the same team that does the BNC traffic reports.

"Now the whole world is going to learn what we already know," says Gilda. "Jamie Grimm? He funny."

"And," adds Gaynor, "he sweat. A lot."

"Perhaps," suggests Pierce, "one of your TV show's first sponsors should be an antiperspirant company."

"Good idea," I say. "I could do a before-and-after deodorant demo. Before, I raise my hand in a classroom..."

"Half the kids keel over from the stench," says Gaynor.

"Exactly. I roll on a little Bye-Bye, BO, and the next time I raise my hand, sweet-smelling wildflowers pop up under everybody's desk."

Gilda smirks. "The janitors are going to love that."

"True. They'll have to mop the floor with a lawnmower."

We're still cracking each other up when Mr. Amodio strides over to say good-bye.

"I have to head back to Hollywood, kid. If you need anything, anything at all, call me. No matter what time. Day or night. But not Sundays. I tan on Sundays."

"Is that why you're so orange?" asks Gaynor innocently.

"It's bronze, kid. *Bronze.*"

Mr. Amodio and his portable news crew choppers off.

"Guess we'd better head back to class," says Gilda. "And after school, I want to brainstorm ideas for my film."

"Awesome," I say.

But then Stewart Johnson, the Hollywood joke machine, pulls up in a sleek black van with dark-tinted windows. It looks like the car Mrs. Vader might use to take her kids to soccer practice.

"Jamie!" he says, practically bursting out of the van, arms thrown open wide. "Got a new joke for ya. You ready?"

"I guess."

"Here it comes. I shot my first turkey this morning. Scared the heck out of everybody else in the frozen-food aisle." He sees my friends. "Who are these three?"

"Gilda Gold, Joey Gaynor, and Jimmy Pierce. My three best buds in the whole world."

"Riiiight," says Johnson. "We're going to work you three into the show. Well, not *you*. Actors pretending to be funnier versions of you."

"Swell," says Gilda, who, if you ask me, is funny enough all by herself. "We need to head back to class."

"Wonderful," says Johnson. "Because I need Jamie."

"But I go to school, too."

Johnson shakes his head. "Not today." He hands me a very official-looking letter with a bumpy seal on the bottom. It's from the Long Beach superintendent of schools. "It's your get-out-of-school-free card, Jamie."

"Um, can I have one of those?" asks Gaynor.

"Win a comedy contest, kid, and we'll talk."

"Come on, you guys," says Gilda, sounding sort of

sad. "I guess we can brainstorm with Jamie some other time. When he's not so busy."

My three best friends walk away.

"I'll text you," I call after them. "We'll find a time…"

"Don't worry about them, kid," says Johnson, putting his hand on my shoulder. "You're with us now."

I nod, even though I'd rather be with my friends.

And Stewart Johnson isn't one of them.

Chapter 19

WRITE OR WRONG?

Stewart Johnson and I head over to the big black van in the parking lot.

When he slides open the side door, I see four guys and one girl inside, all of them clacking away on laptop computers.

"Meet my writing team," says Johnson. "I'd introduce you, but I'm bad with names. Except Bob. I like the name Bob. Any of you guys named Bob?"

They all shake their heads. Without looking up from their keyboards.

"Too bad. Okay, Jamie, here's the plan. We tail you. We tail your three friends and that bully kid."

"Stevie Kosgrov," I say.

"Right. We take notes. We see or hear something funny, we work it into the script."

"I don't know if I want you guys spying on my friends."

"We're not spies, Jamie. We're writers. This is how we do research."

"Or Google," says one of the guys in the van. "We use Google a lot, too."

"Okay, gang," says Johnson, "you know your assignments. Shadow these kids. Keep your eyes and ears open. Write down whatever they say, whatever they do. We want our script to keep it, like the kids say, for realsies."

"Actually," I say, "that's not what *for realsies* means…."

"Well, fo shizzle."

"Um, nobody really says that anymore."

"Then we've got a lot of catching up to do. Okay, team, go do your homework. And when it's time to turn it in, don't tell me your dog ate it!"

A writer follows Stevie Kosgrov around for the next couple of days. Stevie hates it because when Lars Johannsen sees Chip taking notes, he starts terrorizing Stevie even more.

"Be sure you write down this part," Lars says as he's holding Stevie by the ankles over a swirling toilet bowl. "In Minnesota, we call this the Double-Dipsy Dunker Doozie. We usually do it when we're out ice fishing on the lake and get bored staring at the little circle we cut in the ice."

Gaynor *loves* his shadow. He got Emma Smith, a writer he thinks is pretty.

"You'll follow me anywhere?" he asks, sounding love-struck.

Emma Smith shrugs. "It's my job."

"Awesome. So, wanna go to the movies?"

"Sure."

"Wow. Most girls usually say no."

The writer trailing my brainiac buddy Jimmy Pierce fills his entire notebook on day one. Unfortunately, most of it is totally unfunny. Actually, most of it is totally boring.

Did you know that turtles can breathe through their butts?

Me? Well, since I'm supposed to be the star of the show, I get the head writer. Stewart Johnson.

"Hey, Jamie?" he says as we're heading down the sidewalk to Smileyville. "What would happen if you took the bus home from school?"

I shrug. "I don't know. What?"

"The police would make you bring it back! By the way, I found out that shoes are required to eat in the cafeteria. But socks can eat anywhere they like!"

While he's laughing his head off, I'm wondering if I made a mistake signing that contract.

With jokes like those, *Jamie Funnie* isn't going to be very funny, no matter how they spell it.

Chapter 20

SCHOOL DAYS
(IN THIRTY MINUTES OR LESS)

News flash: I have to drop out of school.

Not forever. Just while we're working on the show.

"You're my star," Mr. Amodio says when he calls me from Hollywood to give me the news. "After all, Jamie baby, you're the Planet's Funniest Kid Comic, a phrase that, by the way, is trademarked. If you want to use it, you have to ask me for permission. It's in the fine print, too."

"But," I ask, "how will I keep up with my schoolwork? I mean, I love show business but, well, I'd like to go to college someday. They don't let you in if you're a middle-school dropout."

"Not to worry. We're sending over your new tutor. Her name is Jacqueline Warkentien. The lady's a genius. Works with big-name movie-star kids all the time. She can cram a whole school day's worth of learning into one hour. Fifteen minutes if we're in a pinch. Warkentien's like high-speed Internet, only faster. The limo will be picking you up in five."

"What limo?"

"The one that's hauling you and Ms. Warkentien to the soundstage. It's a thirty-minute ride. You should be able to wrap up your math for the week and learn about Odysseus and his Trojan Horsie, too."

Ms. Warkentien starts tutoring me in the back of the specially equipped SUV limo the instant the chairlift raises me up to door level.

Salutations, young scholar! The average human brain weighs about three pounds. By the time I'm done with yours, it'll weigh a ton. Let's flex those neurons!

Ms. Warkentien's jiggly hand is clutching a tumbler of coffee. Judging by how fast she talks and how much she vibrates, I'm pretty sure it's not decaf.

"Mr. Grimm, I'm Ms. Warkentien, your tutor— from the Old French *tutour* for "guardian," derived from the Latin *tutorem*, a "guardian or watcher," not *tutu*, a stiff skirt worn by ballerinas. You may also call me your teacher, instructor, don, or coach, but not Coach Don. Now that we're done with your vocabulary drill for the day, let's move on to math: pi. Starts with three; decimal places never end. Use it for measuring circles. Time for Shakespeare."

Romeo and Juliet meet. Families fight. Kids date. Kissy face, kissy face. Out come the swords and poison. How tragic. The end.

Since we're knocking off my schoolwork lickety-split, I ask the driver to stop when we reach the corner near the elementary school.

It's recess. The kids have all exploded out the doors and are on the playground swapping jokes.

"I'll just be five minutes," I say.

"Five minutes?" fumes my new tutor. "We could cover the Hundred Years' War in five minutes!"

"I know. But I think this might be more important than any war. Funnier, too."

She relents. The driver gives me the hydraulic-ramp treatment down to the ground.

And for five minutes, I'm right where I want to be: listening to kids who remind me of the me I used to be. Sure, some of the jokes are kind of corny. But they *all* make me smile.

Chapter 21

MEETING MY FAKE BFF

When we reach the soundstage at the Silvercup Studios in Queens, which is just across the river from the bright lights of Manhattan, I've memorized all the Tudor kings and how to figure out the circumference and area of circles.

I roll out of the limo with my head spinning.

"Later," says Ms. Warkentien, "we'll focus on number theory. You know, prime factorization, multiplicative inverses, divisibility rules. Should take five minutes. "

Rose Skye Wilder, the producer I met at school, is there to greet us.

"Good to see you again, Jamie, Ms. Warkentien. Follow me, please. And we're moving, we're moving...."

I roll as fast as I can, trying to keep up with the two fast-moving ladies.

"I've arranged a meet-and-greet inside for you, with Donna Dinkle."

"Sounds great," I say. "Who is she?"

"Only the former star of *Ring My Bell*."

"Sorry. I don't think we get that channel."

"Used to be the number one show with kids in grades three through eight."

"I tutored her," adds Ms. Warkentien. "She never did memorize the periodic table of elements, even though I gave her a whole half hour to do it!"

"Wait a second," I say. "Before Donna Dinkle was a co-star on my show, she was the *star* of her own show? Isn't that, like, a demotion?"

"It happens, Jamie. Word to the wise? The folks you meet on the way up are the same ones you'll meet on the way down."

"It's true," says Ms. Warkentien. "I bump into washed-up former students all the time. Usually at McDonald's. They're always asking me if I want fries with that."

Ms. Wilder and Ms. Warkentien don't break stride as we near the building. I'm pumping my arms like crazy just to keep up. I'm also admiring Silvercup Studios.

"We're moving, we're moving," says Ms. Wilder as I pause to gawk at all the framed posters of famous TV stars from hit shows lining the walls of the lobby.

"Wow. All these people work here?"

"Yes," says Ms. Wilder. "And so does Donna Dinkle, who we really shouldn't keep waiting, Jamie."

"Right. Sorry."

We hurry down a corridor. It's time for me to meet my more-famous-than-me co-star.

JILLDA IS NO GILDA

I follow Ms. Wilder down the hall to the dressing rooms.

Ms. Warkentien heads off to find some coffee, even though, if you ask me, she doesn't need any more caffeine.

Ms. Wilder is still monologuing about Donna Dinkle. (Probably because I spent all that time in the hospital watching classic comedians instead of modern sitcoms.)

"Donna has been in the business since the day she was born. Starred in a series of commercials for Toss 'Ems, the disposable diapers. After that, she moved on to Princess Pony action figures. Then she was the voice of the rutabaga in that 3-D Pixar flick about vegetables. Then she did

Ring My Bell. For four years!"

"And now she's in *my* pilot? Wow."

"Wow is right. We were lucky to land her. That's why her dressing room is slightly larger than yours."

"So, who is Donna playing?" I ask. "One of the teachers at school?"

"She could. She's that talented. But she's only thirteen."

"Oh."

"She'll be playing Jillda."

"Cool. Who's Jillda?"

"Your friend at school. Frizzy hair. Always making movies."

"Oh, you mean Gilda. Gilda Gold."

"The writers changed the name. It's Jillda Jewel now."

"Why?"

"Stewart Johnson says *J* words are funnier than *G* words."

"What about galloping garbanzo beans?"

Before Ms. Wilder can answer, we're inside a huge, flower-filled dressing room.

"Omigosh!" screeches a girl with a mop of curly

hair tucked under a Pittsburgh Pirates baseball cap. She looks exactly like Gilda Gold would look if she were a redhead and didn't love the Boston Red Sox.

"Omigosh!" she gushes. "You're you. You're Jamie, right? You're in a wheelchair and everything, just like when you did your comedy schtick on TV, which, by the way, was, like, total awesomesauce."

103

"It's, uh, an honor to meet you, Miss Dinkle."

"Please, call me Donna. Or Dee Dee. Or Donnatella. I like Donnatella, too."

"Okay. I'll try."

"You know, Jamie, me and Taylor Swift watched you win the Planet's Funniest Kid Comic."

"Seriously?"

"Yuh-huh. Tay-Tay and me were just, you know, hanging out, chillin', watching you kick comedy butt, and I told her I would so totally let you have my handicapped parking space, the one my driver usually snags because it's so close to the doors and everything, even though, you know, technically, my only handicap is being so awesomely famous..."

I know it's hard to believe, but Donna Dinkle, the TV Gilda, is even spunkier than the real one. And she talks nearly as fast as Ms. Warkentien.

"So, Jamie..." Donna sort of wiggles down and grabs hold of both of my armrests. She smells like cinnamon buns at the mall. Best. Perfume. Ever. "Have you been talking to the writers?"

"Little bit" is all I can squeak out, I'm so nervous.

You know that flop sweat I get on stage? It also pops up when I'm close enough to smell a cute girl's

perfume. Yep. She smells terrific, and I smell like the monkey cage at the zoo.

"Have you talked to them about *me?*" Donna purrs.

"Well, no, we only just met and…"

"Not me, silly goose. My character. Jillian."

"Jillda," says Ms. Wilder, who's kind of hovering behind me.

"Whatever," says Donna. "I just want to make sure they write us some tender moments where we share our true feelings for each other."

I gulp a little. "It's, uh, supposed to be a comedy…."

Oh, boy. She's wiggling even closer. She's inches from my face. Batting her eyelashes. Puckering her lips like she's doing a fish impersonation.

"We need to make sure it's a *romantic* comedy. I'd like that….Wouldn't you?"

Chapter 23

BACK TO SCHOOL

While Donna is still lingering inches away from my face (and lips), my jittery tutor, Ms. Warkentien, barges into the dressing room.

"We have ten minutes before they want you on set!" she announces. "We can do American history! The whole enchilada, even though that's not American food. Oh, good, you have a coffeemaker. I emptied the one in the studio. Drank it right out of the pot..."

I don't think she took a single breath while saying that.

She scurries over to the dressing-room counter to fiddle with coffee pods, while Donna Dinkle shows me how well she can emote.

Ms. Wilder checks her watch. "Let's go check out *your* dressing room, Jamie. We're moving, we're moving…"

She basically shoves me out the door and into a dingy closet that, it turns out, is my dressing room. It even smells like mothballs.

"Your bathroom, of course, is handicapped accessible."

"Is it through that door?" I ask.

"No. It's down the hall and to the left. Remember the lobby?"

"Yeah."

"Good. That's where your bathroom is. Enjoy your history lesson."

She leaves. Ms. Warkentien pulls out her textbook.

"Now then, Jamie, the War of 1812. How did it get its name?"

"All the really good war names were already taken?"

"Correct. Let's move on to Mesopotamia and irrigation…."

Fortunately, that's when Uncle Frankie makes his entrance.

"So, Jamie, how's it going?"

"Fantastic. I did about six weeks' worth of school in under an hour, and get this: I met Donna Dinkle."

"You're kidding!"

"Nope. Her dressing room is right next door."

"That's fantastic, kiddo. But tell me something: Who the heck is Donna Dinkle?"

"I'm not sure, but I think she's famous."

Ms. Warkentien packs up her books. Uncle Frankie and I go with Ms. Wilder into Studio B to check out the scenery for the pilot episode.

"Wow," says Uncle Frankie. "My diner looks even better in here than it does on Long Island."

I nod. Everything's a little smaller, a little flatter, but it's super amazing. My whole world is lined up in a row. The diner, Smileyville, the school—interior and exterior—and, of course, a brick wall behind a microphone stand for the comedy club scenes.

It all looks hyper-real.

"How come the scenery's all lined up like that?" asks Uncle Frankie.

"We wanted to make it easy for Jamie to roll from one scene to the next when we do the show live in real time," says Ms. Wilder.

I gulp. "Live?"

"Don't you people usually tape sitcoms?" asks Uncle Frankie.

"True. But Joe Amodio doesn't want *Jamie Funnie* to be business as usual. He wants it to be *big*. So we're launching big. We'll do the pilot live in front of a studio audience—just like they do with *Saturday Night Live*. Sounds great, huh?"

I don't answer right away.

I'm too busy having a panic attack.

Chapter 24

WHEN WRITE BECOMES WRONG

The next day, I roll into the writers' room, where things are really buzzing.

I hope these guys are cooking up some hot 'n' fresh material, because the idea of doing my TV show live is still freaking me out. It means that the whole country will be watching if I make a mistake or something goes wrong. And something *always* goes wrong.

"All right, guys," says the head writer, Stewart Johnson. "Let me hear your best one-liners about school."

He bangs a hotel bell.

The writers start slinging out one-liners.

Nothing's very funny, so I try pitching in.

"How about…"

"Hang on, Jamie," says Johnson. "We're brainstorming. Just spitballing ideas. Seeing what sticks."

"I know, I thought I'd toss in a few ideas. I mean, I wrote all my own material when I won the Planet's Funniest Kid Comic Contest."

"A registered trademark of Joe Amodio Productions," mumble all six writers in unison.

"Okay, Jamie," says Johnson. "Hit us with a zinger."

"Well, I'm not really sure we should be doing 'zingers.' Most of my humor is observational. For instance, how is a kid in a wheelchair supposed to carry books between classes? If I stuff them all in my backpack, maybe my chair would topple over. Books are heavy. And I can't really tuck them under an arm because I need both my arms to power my chair. So, let's say I'm cruising down the hall with books stacked in my lap, and all the other kids think I'm a human library cart, so they start piling more books on top of mine. Then the librarian comes out and hits me with a huge fine because all the books in my lap are overdue."

I raise my eyebrows, awaiting a reaction.

Silence. Dead silence.

"Interesting," says Stewart Johnson with a very slow head bob.

Everybody else just clears their throats. Politely. Emma Smith sharpens her pencil.

I slump down in my seat. Try to disappear.

"How about," says one of the other writers, "Jamie comes to school with a big banana cream pie on his lap? In fact, he brings a dozen pies to school. Maybe two dozen! Banana cream, coconut cream, Bavarian cream..."

"They're all cream pies?" asks Johnson.

"Have to be or the gag doesn't work. Jamie takes his pies to geometry class, where the teacher says that formula...you know the one...for finding the area of a circle..."

"Pi times *r* squared!"

"Bingo! And Jamie shakes his head and tells the teacher, 'No. That's wrong. Cakes are square, pies are round!'"

"And he throws a pie in the teacher's face!" says Emma Smith. "And he has to go to detention hall, and that's where the big pie fight takes place."

Johnson spins around with a big grin on his face. "Whaddaya think, Jamie?"

"Um, a pie fight is kind of Three Stooges–ish."

"You're right. We need seltzer bottles, too!"

The writers spend another half hour milking the pie-fight bit for all the cream and seltzer they can squeeze out of it.

After a quick bathroom break, Stewart Johnson runs a clip from my comedy act on his computer screen.

It's a bit about Stevie Kosgrov.

My cousin Stevie is the biggest bully in my school. Somehow, because I was already in this chair when I moved to town, he thinks I cheated him. "You broke your own legs?" he says to me. "I wanted to do that!"

Jamie FUNNIE!!FINALS! Lol!!
6K views
42 👍 2 👎

Johnson slams down his laptop lid. "That's it! The pilot is all about how Jamie came up with this one bit about the bully."

"What about the pie fight?" asks Chip, the writer who's been shadowing Stevie.

"We save it," says Johnson. "For the second episode. Or maybe season two."

Or maybe never, I'm thinking. Never would work for me.

"I don't know, Stewart," says Chip. "For a bully, this Kosgrov is a real lightweight. Now, there's this other kid, Lars Johannsen. He's huge and hysterical. Yesterday, he stuffed Stevie Kosgrov inside a locker—right after he made Kosgrov gobble down a dozen bean burritos in the cafeteria. Talk about a gas trap."

Johnson springs out of his chair. "Jamie?"

"Yes?"

"We're going on a field trip. We need to go back to school and see Stevie and Lars side by side! We need to pick our bully."

BULLY FOR ME

The writers hoist me up into their van and we head back to Long Beach Middle School.

We pull into the parking lot just as the final bell is ringing. Kids are piling out the doors, running for their buses.

And not a single one of them is being shaken down by Stevie Kosgrov.

"Isn't this prime bullying time?" asks Stewart Johnson.

"Not as big as first thing in the morning," I say, "because everybody's spent their lunch money."

"But wouldn't a first-class bully be out here settling scores and punching people?"

He sounds disappointed that little kids aren't being tortured in front of him.

Finally, we find Stevie sitting on a curb, trying without much enthusiasm to squish a line of ants with a stick.

"Stevie," says Johnson, "we want our TV bully to be just like you. Big. Tough. Nasty. What would you do to threaten Jamie?"

"I don't know. Call him a crip or something."

"Come on, Stevie," urges Emma Smith. "You can do better than that. Show us your stuff."

"It's okay," I tell him. "We're playing it for laughs. Give me a punch so I can give you a punch line!"

Stevie's eyes go wide. I recognize the look. He's choking. Just like I do sometimes when everybody's waiting for me to perform. He's also sweating up a storm. Guess perspiration runs in the family, too.

"What's the matter, Stevie?" snarls a big, nasty voice. "Brain run out of gas? Maybe you need to eat another bean burrito."

It's Lars Johannsen.

"What are you doing here, Funny Boy?" Lars sneers at me.

"Field trip?" I peep.

"Oh, did you come here to see the *fist* exhibit?" He balls up his fist and waggles it in my face. "Well, here it is. In IMAX and 3-D."

He socks me in the stomach.

I go flying backward. When I'm sprawled out like a flopping fish, Lars stomps on that line of ants Stevie was trying to torment. Then he kicks Stevie in the butt.

"Now you have ants in your pants, Kosgrov!"

"Love it!" giggles Emma Smith. "Ants in his pants!"

Lars swaggers away.

None of the writers stop taking notes to help prop me back up. Stevie skulks away, rubbing his sore behind.

Fortunately, Gaynor and Pierce come out of the building just in time to see me spread-eagled and flat on my back.

And, like always, they help me back into my chair while pretending that's not what they're doing.

Chapter 26

ME AND MY FUNNY FRIENDS

The weekend comes and I can finally take a break from prepping the TV pilot.

I can actually spend some time with my real buds, not the actors playing them on TV.

Gaynor, Pierce, Vincent O'Neil, and I all meet at Gilda's house, where we turn her mother's dining room into our own version of the sitcom writing room.

"Is this how the real TV people do it?" asks Vincent eagerly. "They sit around a table just like this one and tell each other jokes and write the show?"

"Sort of," I say. "All the writers toss out ideas. They call it spitballing."

"So," says Gaynor, "do we need, like, straws?"

"No. It's just another way of saying 'brain-storming.'"

"I have an idea," says our resident brainiac, Jimmy Pierce. "Termites have been known to eat food twice as fast when heavy metal music is playing. You could do your movie about that."

"What?" says Gilda. "Jamie plays a termite?"

"Ooh, cool," says Vincent. "We could put antennae on his head!"

"And then I shred my guitar," says Gaynor, jumping into a pretty amazing air-guitar jam complete with rippling fingers, windmilling arms, and thrashing hair.

"You don't play the guitar," says Pierce.

"Doesn't matter. It's heavy metal, man."

"It could be a spoof on an insect video they'd show in science class," I say.

"Spoofs are funny!" says Vincent. "Like in *Mad* magazine."

"I don't know," says Gilda, shaking her head. "Termites?"

"I could eat a box of pencils," I say. "They're wood."

"O-kay," says Gilda. "That's one idea."

"Ooh, oooh," says Vincent. He's so excited, he even raises his hand and waves it at Gilda, the way he always does in class.

"What've you got, Vincent?" she asks.

"What if, instead of spoofing a science video, we do a parody of a driver-education movie? One of those old-school ones!"

"This accident should not have happened," I say in my deepest Highway Patrol Guy voice. "How could it have been avoided?"

Vincent snaps his fingers and points at me. "Exactly."

"Whoa," says Gaynor. "Since Jamie is the star, it could be, like, driver's ed for wheelchairs."

"But the accident," I add, "isn't a wreck."

(I really don't want to make fun of car crashes. Been there. Done that. Wasn't laughing.)

"My accident," I say, "is accidentally running into the school's toughest bully."

"Your cousin Stevie!" says Gilda.

"Or someone dressed like him."

"I could play that part," says Vincent. "I'd just have to slick back my hair and maybe stuff a pillow under my shirt—"

"And," says Gilda, who's totally getting into this idea, "we could shoot the 'accident' in slow motion like they do with crash-test dummies."

"But," I say, "since you're a student director, we pretend you can't afford real slow motion—"

"So we have to act out everything in fake slow-mo like a bad stop-motion dinosaur battle in a cheesy horror flick," says Vincent.

"But," says Pierce, "while you two are moving as slowly as you can and slurring your words like you're even talking in slow motion, we have some people walk through the background at normal speed—"

"And," I say to Gilda, "you could keep coaching us. We do the same scene over and over. We shoot you giving us directions. Slower, faster, happier, sadder…"

Gilda's eyes sparkle. "It's a film about directing a film!"

You guys are wackaloons!
I LOVE wackaloons!

And the ideas keep tumbling out of all of us. The bit keeps getting bigger and funnier. I toss out a few funny one-liners. So does Vincent O'Neil. There are no pie fights or seltzer-bottle battles, but we're cracking each other up.

Gilda is so psyched, she kisses all four of us.

And I realize something: Being funny is a lot more fun when you do it for laughs instead of money.

Chapter 27

KILLING FOR A GOOD CAUSE

Saturday night, Uncle Frankie and I do an appearance for a literacy charity on Long Island called Books of Hope.

The event is held in a huge hotel ballroom. One thousand people pay a ton of money to hear me tell a few jokes and to watch Uncle Frankie twirl his yo-yo. All the money will be used to buy books for kids who otherwise wouldn't have anything to read except Happy Meal boxes at McDonald's.

Uncle Frankie warms everybody up with an impressive display of tricks including a Pop 'n' Fresh, a couple of Boingy Boings, and his big finish, the Man on the Flying Trapeze. That one starts on his left, loops around, and lands on his right. And he does it blindfolded. He flings a double Lindy Loop when he takes his bows.

Then it's my turn.

"Ladies and gentlemen," booms a big voice from the ceiling speakers. He sounds a lot like the guy who announces the WWF wrestlers on TV. "Please put your hands together for the Planet's Funniest Kid Comic, Long Island's own, soon to be the star of his own sitcom on BNC-TV, the one and only Jay-meeeeee Griiiiiiiimmmmmmmmm!"

I've never heard anyone take so long to say my name.

I roll up a ramp to the stage and tell a bunch of the jokes I'm famous for. I slay 'em.

Since I'm killing it big-time and the audience is totally with me, I try out a new joke about battling bullies that I'm hoping I can sneak into the script for the TV pilot.

"A boy I know was being picked on by a bully at school," I say, gripping the microphone with both hands. "So his father hired a boxing coach to help the kid out. Two weeks later, he knocked out the bully with one punch. The father and son just sat on their bench and laughed."

The audience is howling.

"Thank you, ladies and gentlemen! And thanks for helping so many good kids get good books to read!"

I wave to the crowd and roll down my ramp.

Where I practically run over Cool Girl.

"You were terrific, Jamie."

"Thanks."

"So remember this night. This is what it's all about."

I arch an eyebrow. "Telling jokes in hotel ballrooms while people eat dessert?"

"You know what I mean." She points to the big pictures of smiling kids with books that are displayed all around the ballroom. "The doing is its own reward."

I sometimes wonder if Cool Girl is my own much more attractive, less wrinkly Yoda—here to give me words of wisdom.

"Hey, Jamie." Uncle Frankie bustles over to join us. "We're a hit. The charity folks want us back."

"Here?"

"No. The Long Beach Public Library. A bunch of kids from the Books of Hope program meet to work on their reading skills. They want us to do lunch with the kids, give 'em a special treat."

"But what about the TV pilot? They may not let me out of rehearsal."

Cool Girl gives me a very chilly look. So I keep going.

"But if those people try something dumb like that," I say with all the bluster I can muster, "well, I'll just tell them I'm the star and they have to work around *my* schedule."

Uncle Frankie claps me on the back. "That's the spirit, Jamie!"

As for Cool Girl's reaction, let's just say Yoda is smiling again.

I guess I'm a better actor than I thought.

Chapter 28

WHO ARE THESE PEOPLE?

On Monday, Uncle Frankie, Ms. Warkentien, and I take the Hummer limo back to Silvercup Studios.

My tutor tries to teach Uncle Frankie the entire history of the yo-yo in sixty seconds or less.

"A terra-cotta yo-yo from fifth-century Greece is on display in Greece's national museum. Hunters in the Philippines hid in trees and used yo-yo rocks with cords twenty feet long to slay beasts on the ground. It was a fashionable toy for French nobility, many of whom used their yo-yos to relieve stress as they walked to the guillotine...."

Unfortunately, we don't get to hear the rest. We're needed on set.

It's time to meet the rest of the cast—the actors who will be playing Uncle Frankie, the Smileys, and all my friends at school. I have a funny feeling Meryl Streep and Brad Pitt won't be there. Or The Rock.

I'm wondering if the actors who *are* there will be as experienced (and as weird) as Donna Dinkle. I didn't have any say over the casting, which I guess makes sense since I've never done it before. Still, for a show that has my name on it, I feel awfully left out of the whole thing.

As we roll through the Silvercup lobby, a man carrying coffee in a paper cup comes over to introduce himself.

"Great to meet you, Jamie," he says. "I'm Richard Wetmore. I'm going to be the booth director on your pilot."

"There's a booth in the show?" I ask.

"A phone booth?" adds Uncle Frankie. "And it needs directions?"

Mr. Wetmore smiles. "No. I'm going to be the frantic guy in the control booth calling the camera shots. Since this is a live show, Brad Grody will be handling the artistic end of things on the floor while I take care of all the less glamorous technical details upstairs."

Uncle Frankie whistles. "Sounds like a pretty high-pressure job."

"It is. But don't worry, Jamie, I can handle it. In fact, I'll do everything I can to make sure your show is the best it can possibly be. My daughter, Serena, is a huge fan."

And then he tells us about her cerebral palsy.

How she's confined to a wheelchair.

How I make her laugh.

How I give her hope.

I'm about to start sobbing. Uncle Frankie already is.

"You're her hero, Jamie," says Mr. Wetmore. "And that makes you *my* hero, too."

I sign an autograph for Mr. Wetmore to take home to Serena, and then Uncle Frankie and I head into Studio B to meet the rest of the cast.

"Boy," says Uncle Frankie, "I can't wait to see what I look like!"

MY INCREDIBLE
SHRINKING FRIENDS

It turns out that Nigel Bigglebottom, the actor playing Uncle Frankie, looks just like him. Sounds like him, too, except when he's not in character. Then he sounds very British.

Righty-o, Francis. What say you, old bean? Shall we nip out for a spot of tea and crumpets?

I'm not big on crumpets. What are crumpets, anyway?

"I can teach you how to twirl that yo-yo," Uncle Frankie tells Nigel.

"Splendid!"

They head off to practice Walking the Dog while the director, Brad Grody, introduces me to everybody else.

"You're going to love your groovy new family and friends, Jamie."

Hi!

Hi!

Hiss!

Hi!

Hey, J.

Hi!

...Hi!

MRS. FROWNIE

MR. FROWNIE

JILLDA JEWEL

FROWNIE #2

JAMIE?

These "groovy" smiling Smileys are freaking me out!

"You've already met Jillda Jewel, chya?"

"Um, yes."

Donna Dinkle bats her eyelashes at me. I can smell her cinnamon-bun perfume from twenty paces away.

"Did you talk to the writers?" she whispers so loudly they can probably hear her back in Long Beach.

"Um, not yet."

She pouts.

"But I'm going to!"

She smiles.

She's good. She can change her whole attitude faster than most people blink.

"Next," says Mr. Grody, "we have the four freaky Frownies."

"You mean the Smileys."

"*F* words are always funnier, little dude. If you don't believe me, talk to Stewart Johnson."

"Right."

"We're looking forward to not laughing at anything you say, do, or think," says the actor playing Mr. Frownie.

"Thanks," I say. "Appreciate it."

"And," says Grody, "instead of a crappuccino dog, we gave them a grumpy cat."

"You got Grumpy Cat?" I say. "The Internet sensation?"

"No, bro. GC wanted his own private litter box. We picked up Frownie Cat in an alley behind the studio. She'll work for kibble.

"And, of course," continues Grody, "here's your tormentor. Our bully, Lars from Mars."

"What about Stevie Kosgrov?"

"This is totes awk, Jamie, but your stepbro didn't make the cut. The real Lars, on the other hand—whoa, that blond Viking dude is flipping cray-cray. Gives us more to work with. And, last but not least, meet Bob."

"Hi," I say to the boy who's wearing a porkpie hat and has a nose ring.

Then I turn to Mr. Grody.

"Who's Bob?" I whisper.

"Your best bud. We took those goofballs Gaynor and Pierce and squished them together to make one character. We save money that way."

"B-b-but—"

"It'll be better, little dude. Trust me. Less of them means more of you."

I nod.

Even though inside, I'm already missing my two real friends.

Chapter 30

PUTTING IT ON ITS FEET
(THE SCRIPT, NOT ME)

After the introductions, we all sit down around a square of cafeteria-sized folding tables to read through the first draft of the script.

I think Johnson and his team worked over the weekend. The script is actually pretty good now, which is a huge relief. Much better than I thought it would be. And nobody gets creamed in the face with a pie.

Mr. Wetmore, the tech director, starts us off by reading out the stage directions.

"Interior. Comedy club. We open on Jamie in a bright spotlight in front of a brick wall. He rolls up to the microphone and launches into his bully routine."

I've marked all my lines with a neon-yellow highlighter. The whole first page of the script is all yellow. It's just me.

"And cue Jamie," says Brad Grody, doing a karate chop in my direction.

I launch into my monologue about bullies.

"Y'know, my school has these NO BULLYING ZONE posters hanging all over the place. Outside every classroom. Up and down the halls. Only one problem: Bullies aren't big readers. Reading's not really a job requirement in the glamorous field of Wedgie Yanking. So, I have a better idea: reverse psychology. No more posters. Instead, every time a bully dunks a kid's head in a toilet, a teacher gives that bully a gold star. The principal congratulates him during announcements: 'Way to go, Lars. Nice work on that Triple Nipple Cripple.' Before long, the bully gets a reputation as a kiss-up and teacher's pet. He has no choice but to cram his own head down a toilet and flush!"

The tables erupt with laughter. As always, it makes me want to keep going. Laughs are like potato chips. Once you have one, you want another.

I read my next lines.

"This one bully at my middle school, a big blond dude we call Lars from Mars, makes you eat a half dozen bean burritos in the cafeteria before he locks you inside your locker. Know why? Well, there's very little ventilation in that tight metal box. Plus, the metal walls make the farts echo like crazy."

More laughs. Even a couple of guffaws. I love guffaws.

"And fade to black," says Mr. Wetmore.

The rest of the cast applauds.

"Way to go, Jamie," gushes Donna Dinkle. "That was super-duper awesometastic."

"I loooooved what you did with it, kiddo," says Grody. "Like Donna said, it was awesometastic."

"Stupendilicious," says Stewart Johnson.

"I loved how you said my character's name," says the giant playing Lars from Mars.

It takes, like, five minutes for the whole cast to tell me how much they loooove me.

Both Uncle Frankies seem pleased.

Me?

I have to be honest: I absolutely love all the loooooove.

Chapter 31

THE PERKS OF BEING A TV STAR

Things are going so well, we wrap early.

And for the first time since Mr. Amodio landed his helicopter on the middle school ball field, I'm feeling good about the show. Maybe my dream really can come true. And if this one can, so can all my others. Except the one about the unicorn that brings me chocolate-covered marshmallows. That's probably still a long shot.

It's great to be a big-time TV star when I arrive home in Long Beach and bump into the real Lars Johannsen. The blond giant is so wide, he blocks the whole sidewalk. He kind of reminds me of Thor, but without the hammer.

"I hear you're making fun of me on your TV show."

"Not you," I say. "Lars from Mars."

"I'm not from Mars. I told you, I'm from Minnesota."

> Tell you what, Lars. How about tomorrow we switch places? **YOU** go star in a TV show, and **I'll** go act like a jerk.

While I'm boldly cracking wise, Lars makes low, rumbling *grrrrr* noises. He sounds like a German shepherd right before it locks its jaws around your leg and sinks in its teeth.

It doesn't scare me. I keep going. Lars keeps growling.

"The TV people are paying me to act like a fool. What's your excuse?"

I can tell Lars is thinking about the best way to rip my head off.

"You're kind of blocking the way," I say. "And I refuse to engage in a battle of wits with someone who doesn't have any weapons." I give him a little "shoo" wave.

He steps aside. I roll on by, grinning.

Like I said earlier, comedy is one surefire way to beat a bully.

Another is to have two beefy bodyguards assigned to your personal security detail while you're working on a TV pilot for Joe Amodio.

So, um, can you guys stick with me for the rest of my life?

Chapter 32

LAUGHING TILL IT HURTS

That night, Aunt Smiley helps me rehearse my lines.

Alert the media! Aunt Smiley is actually **_smiling_**!

"This is funny, Jamie," she says. "But who are these Frownie people?"

I shrug. "A family the writers made up."

"They're so odd. They never seem to smile. Even when you're cracking all these funny jokes."

"I know, they're so weird."

"And this Lars character is so mean. He makes Stevie look like an angel."

"I'm no angel!" Stevie shouts from his bedroom down the hall.

"Oh, look," I say loud enough for Stevie to hear, "here comes Lars Johannsen."

"I'm not home!" Stevie screams. Then he slams his door shut.

"Is someone coming up the walkway?" asks Mrs. Smiley.

"No. I was just practicing my acting."

"Oh. That was good. I thought you really saw somebody."

Yep. And so did Stevie.

After we go through all my scenes two or three more times, Aunt Smiley puts down the script and sighs.

"You know, Jamie," she says softly, "more than anything, I wish your mom and dad were here to see how well you're doing. Little Jenny, too. She'd be so excited. Her big brother, a TV star…"

All I can do is nod. If I try to speak, I'll just start bawling my eyes out.

"Jamie? Have I told you lately how proud we all are of everything you've accomplished?"

I shake my head.

"Well, we are. They would be, too."

We sit there silently, each of us remembering that horrible night on the rain-slicked highway. It seems so long ago. And like it only happened yesterday.

We're both remembering the car wreck on the side of the mountain that made it impossible for me to walk and then did something even worse.

It made me an orphan.

It took away my baby sister.

"I'm so glad you found comedy, Jamie," says Aunt Smiley, sniffling back her tears. "They say laughter is the best medicine. I think they might be right."

Me too.

Making people laugh eases the pain. It doesn't take it away. Nothing can do that. But it sure helps me keep going.

And when I'm in the spotlight, blinded by its

brightness, when I can't see anything but a hazy funnel of white, I think my mom and dad and Jenny can see me, no matter how far away they might be.

Aunt Smiley reaches across the table and pats my hand.

"Don't worry, Jamie. They'll see your show. There must be TV in heaven. HBO and cable, too. They probably have *all* the channels—even the ones that nobody really watches."

Chapter 33

PRACTICE MAKES PERFECT... AND PERSPIRATION

We rehearse all week.

Brad Grody shows me how to "hit my marks," which means where to park my wheelchair to deliver my lines so the cameras can see me.

The other actors are pretty amazing. Nigel Bigglebottom cracks me up as Uncle Frankie.

Then, whenever we take a break, he cracks me up even more as Uncle Frankie with a British accent.

The only slight problem is Jillda Jewel, my TV Gilda.

Donna Dinkle keeps improvising lines that aren't in the script, and Brad Grody, the director, doesn't correct her. I guess because Donna's such a big-deal TV star. Actually, Grody doesn't do much directing at all. He spends most of his time sending out tweets, especially when we're rehearsing the Jillda scenes.

For instance, after Lars from Mars decks me on the sidewalk in front of the school and Bob (my hybrid Pierce and Gaynor) helps me back into my chair, Jillda is supposed to say, "Are you okay, Jamie?" I'm supposed to tell her, "I'm okay, but I think I have a wad of bubble gum in my hair." Then Bob says, "Oh, that's mine. I spit it out earlier." That's when the audience will hopefully laugh.

But instead of saying her line, Donna Dinkle sort of ruins the bit by ad-libbing, "Did that hurt, Jamie? Can I kiss it to make it better? I know kissing you would make *me* feel better. A whole lot better."

Finally, from the booth, Mr. Wetmore, the tech director, calls, "Cut." His voice is tinny, coming out of speakers up in the light grid over the set.

"Brad?" he says.

Finally, Grody puts down his smartphone. I was wrong. He wasn't tweeting. He was playing Candy

Crush Saga.

"Yo, Rich, my man," says Grody. "What's the problem, bro?"

"This show will be going out live. If we keep adding lines, we'll never finish on time."

Donna Dinkle props her hands on her hips and looks up at the ceiling where Mr. Wetmore's voice is coming from.

"I'm improvising," she protests. "We did it all the time on *Ring My Bell*."

"This isn't *Ring My Bell*," replies Mr. Wetmore.

"You're darn right it's not. *Ring My Bell* was a huge hit!"

And then she storms off the set.

Mr. Grody tells everybody to "take five," as in a five-minute break. "I need to see if our star is okay," he says, going after Donna.

Funny. I thought I was the star of *Jamie Funnie*. Guess I was wrong.

MY FANS ROLL IN!

When Donna storms off, the other actors and I are sort of stranded on the set, along with the whole crew.

"Wonder what would happen if *you* walked off the set like that," says Michael McKee, the actor who plays Bob.

"It'd be a major medical miracle," I crack.

Half an hour later, Donna and Mr. Grody come back, all smiles.

"Donna and I had a chill chat," says Grody. "And she's right. We need to pump some air into this bicycle tire, see if it has bounce. We need to run this show in front of a live studio audience."

A live audience, this early in rehearsals? Right

away, I feel anxious. I look over at Donna, who winks back smugly.

"So that's what we're going to do," says Grody. "Tomorrow. We'll invite our first audience. Friends, associates, colleagues. We'll see how they react to our rehearsal. It'll be a great chance to find out what's working in the script and what's not."

The next day, when Uncle Frankie and I pull into the Silvercup parking lot, we see this long line of people waiting to come in and watch us run through the show. I feel a lot better when I see who they are.

A lot of the kids are in wheelchairs.

I think that's pretty cool. So I work the line and sign a bunch of autographs.

"Hey, Jamie," says one kid. "I voted for you on TV!"

"Me too!" shrieks a girl. "I love you, Jamie."

"Well," I say, "I love you guys."

Richard Wetmore, the technical director, comes over. "Serena wanted to be here, but she had something after school."

"Next time," I say.

"Definitely," says Mr. Wetmore. We fist-bump on it.

"Whoa, whoa, whoa." Brad Grody comes barreling out the front door. "Who are all these cripple kids, bro?"

You ever hear a dozen people gasp at the same time?

None of us can believe what Mr. Grody just said.

"This isn't some sort of charity telethon," snaps Grody.

"They're audience members," says Mr. Wetmore. "Fans of Jamie's. I tweeted about the sneak preview to some of my daughter's friends."

"This show is supposed to be funny. These kids make it look sad."

"They're in the audience, Brad," says Mr. Wetmore. "Our cameras aren't pointed at them. We *hear* the audience, we don't *see* them."

"Fine. But keep it that way. Joe Amodio will be watching today's run-through out in LA. I don't want to depress him with an audience that looks like a hospital ward."

Grody goes back inside.

Mr. Wetmore puts his hand on my shoulder. Addresses the kids. "Don't worry, guys. I'll make sure we put extra microphones down front where you'll be sitting. We want your laughs to be louder than anybody else's. Right, Jamie?"

"Definitely!" I say.

The kids all applaud.

"Come on, Jamie," says Mr. Wetmore. "Let's head

inside and give your fans a great show—the kind they deserve!"

I'm feeling totally pumped. "Let's do it!" I pop a wheelie and hop the curb.

And as we head to my dressing room, I can't help thinking that I wish Mr. Wetmore was on the floor, directing the show, and that Brad Grody was the one in the booth.

A tollbooth.

On the New Jersey Turnpike.

Chapter 35

YES, I'M A GUY
AND I WEAR MAKEUP

A makeup lady comes into my dressing room and starts slathering what she calls "foundation" all over on my face.

It isn't concrete and cinder blocks. It's orangish gunk so I "don't wash out" under the lights.

My co-star Donna Dinkle swoops into my dressing room from her much larger room next door.

"Gosh! Our first time putting the show on its feet in front of a live studio audience."

"Actually," I say, "I plan on remaining seated the whole time."

Donna ignores my little quip because I was the one who said it, not her.

"I bet you're nervous," she says. "I know I would be. I remember my first run-through with a live audience. I was *sooooo* scared. All those people packed into the bleachers, staring at me. Waiting for me to say or do something funny..."

Now that Donna mentions it, maybe I should be a little more nervous.

"I thought I was going to die!" Donna continues. "Really. I did. So much pressure."

I tug at my collar. "Yeah..."

"And, of course, Joe Amodio is going to be

watching the run-through out in Hollywood."

"I know." Yes, my voice is cracking.

The makeup lady powder-puffs my face to blot away the flop sweat that just drizzled out of my hair.

I'll either die of stage fright in front of the camera or drown in my own sweat right here.

Someone turn off this kid's pores or bring me a mop!

Okay. I'm not just nervous anymore. Now I'm petrified. Like those trees that turned into rocks out in Arizona. Ms. Warkentien taught me about those. She even showed me a picture. For two seconds.

The first time I ever appeared in front of a live audience on Long Island, I totally choked. All I could remember were my punch lines. I'd forgotten all the setups. "An investigator!" isn't exactly funny if you don't say "What do you call an alligator in a vest?" first.

The makeup lady packs up her gear and leaves just as Brad Grody sticks his head in my dressing room door.

"Yo, Jamie, Donna—you two ready to rock?"

"You bet, BG," chirps Donna.

All I can get out is, "Um…I…uh…hummina…"

Donna takes Mr. Grody's elbow and leads him out of my dressing room. "I have an idea, BG…."

When they're down the hall, I think Donna is telling Grody something like, "If Jamie bombs, I could take his place. I know how to operate a wheelchair."

I can't be sure.

I'm so freaked out, my ears aren't working very well. They feel like clogged echo chambers. On the plus side, if I go deaf, maybe I can score a second handicapped sticker for Uncle Frankie's van.

Chapter 36

HELLO? WHO AM I?

I'm so out of it, one of the stagehands has to wheel me onto the set.

He parks me in front of the fake brick wall of the comedy club. He adjusts the microphone stand.

I just sit there, trying to remember my name.

And why all these people are staring at me.

I see those kids in the wheelchairs down front. My fans. Their smiles are so huge.

Behind them, on risers, is an audience of maybe two hundred other people. I see the real Gilda, Gaynor, and Pierce. Vincent O'Neil waves at me. Uncle Frankie is off to the side of the bleachers, twirling his yo-yo. It's what he does whenever he gets nervous.

Just like those French guys walking to the guillotine!

That means there must be something to be nervous about.

"Cameras up," calls Mr. Wetmore from the ceiling speakers. "We're live in five, four, three…"

A crew member counts down the seconds with his fingers.

When he hits *one*, he points at me.

That locomotive beacon of a spotlight thumps on. I'm not just blinded, I'm also struck dumb.

This is worse than that first performance in front of an audience. I can't remember *anything*. Not a single punch line or setup, or even whether I remembered to put on underpants this morning.

I sit there. Stunned.

The audience is stunned, too. They came to see *Jamie Funnie*, not *The Silence of the Jamie*.

Suddenly, I hear Mr. Wetmore, whispering from the rafters.

"Y'know, my school has these NO BULLYING ZONE posters…"

I wonder why Mr. Wetmore is telling me about the posters at his school. Then I wonder, *Why is he still going to school?* He looks to be thirty or forty years old. He should've graduated a long time ago.

"They're hanging all over the place," he says.

Finally, I realize that's what *I'm* supposed to say. He's giving me my line. So I say it.

"They're hanging all over the place."

The audience stares.

A couple of people grunt, "Huh?" and "What?"

Can't really blame 'em. What I just said makes absolutely no sense.

Now I hear people clearing their throats. Others are squirming in their seats. I'm squirming in mine, too. This goes on for, like, sixty seconds—the longest minute in the history of the universe. It's not exactly what you would call Must-See TV.

"Cut," shouts Brad Grody. "Stop the feed. Hollywood says pull the plug."

I hear a click in the ceiling. "Let's give Jamie another chance," pleads Mr. Wetmore.

"No can do. Mr. Amodio is a busy man," says Grody.

The house lights come up. I see the disappointment in the faces of all those wheelchair kids down front, the ones who were going to laugh the loudest.

"I'm sorry," I mumble as they all silently head toward the exits.

That's when Donna Dinkle decides to come on set and give me her opinion, too.

"I thought you were supposed to be funny."

"Yeah," I say. "I thought so, too."

PART TWO
All That Glitters

Chapter 37

THE SECOND-WORST DAY OF MY LIFE

I sit silently in the fake comedy club as the audience streams out.

This is starting to feel like the second-worst day of my life. (It would be the absolute worst day of my life, but that already took place when I lost my family. It will never be topped, no matter how long I live.)

I just shake my head when Uncle Frankie and my friends ask if I'm okay. They know me pretty well, so they nod and leave me alone.

When it's just me and my wheelchair sitting in the semidarkness, Mr. Wetmore comes strolling onto the set.

"How you doing, Jamie?" he asks.

"I've had better days," I say. "In fact, only one has ever been worse."

"Hey, this sort of thing happens. That's why I made a few phone calls."

"To who? Professional carpet cleaners to come remove the sweat stains from my costume?"

Mr. Wetmore smiles. "No. My pals over at *Saturday Night Live*. I used to work at 30 Rock in the control booth. That's why Joe Amodio wanted me in the booth for your show. I'm familiar with handling live broadcasts and all their unexpected surprises."

"Like the main character forgetting his lines?"

He nods. "One time, I remember Jacky Hart was doing this bit…"

"You know Jacky Hart? She's, like, the funniest person on *SNL*."

"Well, we gave her the wrong cue cards. She was costumed for the cat sketch, but we had the cards up for the roller-derby number."

"What did she do?"

"Winged it. Created one of the most hilarious *SNL* bits ever—"

"The roller-skating cats. I loved that! The way they argued about which cat would make the best YouTube video…"

"Well, Jacky loves you, too, Jamie. Wants you to be a special surprise guest star on the show tomorrow. They're messengering over a script."

"What? Me? On *SNL*?"

"It's a live show, Jamie. Just like the one we're gonna do. I figured it might be a good way for you to work through your nerves."

"B-b-but…"

"Don't worry. Jacky Ha-Ha will be out there with you."

"Who's Jacky Ha-Ha?"

"That's what everybody at *SNL* calls Jacky Hart. Long story. Maybe she'll tell it to you sometime. Anyway, Jacky is a real pro. Her motto is 'Every mistake is just a chance to do something even funnier.' If you freeze, she'll thaw you out."

"But today's Friday. I won't have time to memorize my lines by tomorrow."

"You don't really have to. They'll all be written out for you on cue cards. Whaddaya say? Jacky really wants you on the show."

I think about it for a second.

Mr. Wetmore is right. Doing a live show with the pros might help me get rid of some of my jitters about doing a live show of my own. And with the way my acting career is starting off, this chance might never come around again.

"Okay," I say. "Let's do it."

"That's the spirit. I'll let Jacky know."

I nod.

And hope *my* cue cards don't get mixed up with the ones from Jacky Ha-Ha's old cat sketch.

Chapter 38

FRIDAY NIGHT DEAD

Jacky Hart and the people at *Saturday Night Live* send me a script for a hilarious sketch. I read it on the ride home to Smileyville.

It's fantastic. A five-minute bit about alien comedians coming to Earth to challenge me to a joke duel because they've heard that I'm the funniest kid comic on the planet. Jacky Hart plays the host for the interplanetary joke-off, but she does it as her most famous character, Priscilla the Prude, and that makes the whole scene even funnier.

Feeling better than I have all week, I roll up the ramp into Casa Smiley. I want to grab a quick snack in the kitchen and then head to the garage to run my lines for the *SNL* bit.

Maybe today's disaster on set was just a one-time fluke, especially after listening to Donna Dinkle's anti–pep talk. After all, when I was in the Planet's Funniest Kid Comic Contest, I performed in front of a huge auditorium of people—and I won!

All of a sudden, I'm totally pumped about doing a live show. I've always done my best work in front of an audience. I feed off their energy. When it sounds like the whole world is laughing with me, it makes me feel, I don't know, funnier. Laughter puts me in the zone.

I just wish someone would put Stevie Kosgrov in a zone, too.

A tow-away zone.

Because when I get home, I hear Stevie in his room. He's snorting and laughing and having a great time. I figure he's in there slaying some more helpless zombies on his Xbox.

But then I hear another voice.

A voice with a thick Midwestern accent, don'tcha know.

It's Lars Johannsen.

Oh, no. My two worst nightmares have become one!

"Dumping the crip into a trash barrel is a two-person job," Stevie tells Lars. "I couldn't pull it off by myself."

Lars smiles. Even his teeth are huge. "That's why I'm here, Stevie! Come on. We need to practice our moves...."

I can't believe this.

Bullies rehearse, too? Amazing.

But I've got to be honest: The thought of Stevie Kosgrov and Lars Johannsen joining forces and ganging up on me is pretty terrifying. It's like the Joker teaming up with Lex Luthor. Doctor Doom with Mister Sinister. These two are definitely the Injustice League.

I roll down the hall and take the ramp to the garage. You can bet I'm locking the dead bolt and using the door chain tonight.

As for tomorrow night…maybe Mr. Amodio will let me bring home one of those bodyguards.

Chapter 39

SAYING HI-HI TO HA-HA

This is amazing," says Uncle Frankie as the limo drops us off outside 30 Rockefeller Center, the home of *Saturday Night Live* and *The Tonight Show Starring Jimmy Fallon*.

Hey, look, Uncle Frankie! The Umbrella Club is still open, just like the last time we were here!

Not too long ago, Uncle Frankie treated us all to *Saturday Night Live* tickets and a gourmet hot-dog dinner on the street. I can't believe we're back in Manhattan because I'm going to be a special guest star. On *SNL*, not at the wiener cart.

It's about four in the afternoon. Jacky Hart wants to go over the script with me a few times before the eight PM dress rehearsal (in front of a live studio audience) and then the eleven thirty PM live broadcast (in front of bajillions of people). We're going to meet her up on the seventeenth floor, where *SNL* has its offices.

We roll into the lobby.

"Hey, Jamie!"

OMG. It's Jimmy Fallon. I was a guest on his *Tonight Show* before the finals of the Planet's Funniest Kid Comic Contest. I can't believe he actually recognizes me.

"Heard you were doing *SNL* tonight," he says to me. "Have fun!"

He says good-bye, and some security guards show us which elevator to take up to the seventeenth floor.

The place is humming like a beehive. About

fifty people are bustling around. Some trying on costumes. Some nibbling sandwiches. Others waving script pages and toting props.

"Jamie?"

It's Jacky Hart. She has two girls with her, both about my age.

"These are my daughters, Tina and Grace. They're huge fans."

"So am I," I say, trying not to stammer.

"No," says Jacky, "they're *your* fans, Jamie. Not mine. I'm their mother. Moms don't have many fans in their own family."

The two girls roll their eyes. The way daughters everywhere do when their moms embarrass them in public.

"You know," Jacky says to me, "when I was your age, I was climbing Ferris wheels down on the Jersey shore."

I do a comic arch of an eyebrow. "Hmmm," I say nonchalantly. "Don't think I'll be doing that anytime soon."

And instead of getting all gushy and apologizing for being politically incorrect, Jacky Hart just laughs. "Good one!"

I like this lady. I like her a lot.

Chapter 40

LIVE FROM NEW YORK, IT'S ME!

We rehearse in the big conference room.

We rehearse on the stage.

We dress-rehearse in front of a live audience.

It's fun. The alien-comic bit is a hit.

Jacky Hart gives me a few pointers, tells me I'm doing great, and then, at eleven thirty on the dot, *Saturday Night Live* is on the air. And we're the first act, the cold opening.

My costume is simple. I look like me. My chair looks like my chair.

Jacky Hart, however, has transformed into Priscilla the Prude. Tina Fey, the guest host for the night, is playing one of the alien comics. She has deely-bopper antennae bouncing around over her head and is pretending to be Princess Galactica from the planet Poingo Boingo.

A funny guy from the *SNL* cast named Charlie Garner is playing Chameleon the Comedian from a planet called Kaizuka. He's wearing a lizard costume and a sparkly silver tuxedo space suit.

The three of us sit behind game-show contestant desks. Jacky Hart stands behind a podium.

Jacky Hart is hilarious. Her character, Priscilla the Prude, over e-nun-ci-ates every word she says. She also looks down her nose a lot.

"Welcome to the Funniest Kid Comic in the Universe Contest. Let's meet our contestants. Jamie Grimm, who, theoretically, is the funniest kid comic on the planet Earth."

"I have the trophy to prove it," I say, nailing my first line.

"Did you bring it with you, young man?"

"No. Sorry. Couldn't carry it and work my wheels at the same time."

The crowd laughs. Jacky, in full prude mode, scowls at them, too.

"We also have Princess Galactica, the funniest child comedian on the planet Poingo Boingo."

Tina Fey does a Spock salute. "Live long and prosper. Until I destroy you."

"And our final contestant, from the planet Kaizuka, Chameleon the Comedian."

Charlie Garner, underneath his giant lizard costume, launches into a cheesy Vegas routine.

"Hey, great to be here. I just flew five thousand light-years, and boy, is my tail tired."

"Um, you mean your arms," I say, trying to help him out.

"Negative. On my planet, we flap our tails."

The audience laughs.

"Thank you," the lizard says to the audience. "I love you, too. I mean that. I do. From the bottom of my lizard gizzard."

"His joke is complete," says Tina Fey in a robotic alien voice. "It is my turn."

"Very well," says Jacky. "Proceed, please." She pronounces both *p*'s so properly, she sort of sprays them.

"Whoa," says the lizard. "And I thought *I* was a flying-spit machine."

Tina Fey grabs a microphone off the desk and works it like a stand-up comedian. "A Zizznat, a Flaggle, and a Hadorphian Mulchmumpher walk into a bar—"

"I'm sorry," says Jacky. "No one on Earth knows what those things are."

Tina Fey raises a funny-looking Super Soaker. It blinks and warbles. "Allow me to complete my amusing recitation."

"Fine," Jacky says to Tina, acting scared. "Give us your punch line."

"Very well. They walk into a bar. It hurts. For the bar is made of Tilarium steel. It is quite comical."

"I see…" says Jacky.

"You are not laughing."

"Probably because it wasn't funny."

Tina raises her warbling Super Soaker again.

Jacky pretends to panic. "It wasn't funny, it was *hysterical*. Moving on. Jamie?"

"Yes, ma'am?"

"Your joke, if you please?"

I straighten up in my chair. "A bear walks into a restaurant and tells the waitress, 'I'll have a hamburger and…'"

I wait about three seconds, just like Jacky coached me.

"'…French fries.' The waitress says, 'Why the big pause?' The bear looks at his hands. 'I don't know. I've just always had them.'"

The crowd cracks up. Jacky Hart shoots me a wink. I turn to the camera.

"And then the bear says, 'Live from New York, it's Saturday night!'"

The band starts wailing.

The audience starts applauding.

And I start feeling funny again.

Chapter 41

DOING A DOUBLE TAKE

You want to know how good a friend Gilda Gold is?

On Monday morning, she's willing to skip school so she can come with me to Silvercup Studios and another day of rehearsal for *Jamie Funnie*, which, I have to say, I'm feeling much better about doing live now that I have the *SNL* sketch under my belt.

Luckily, Gilda's a pretty good actress and can fake a stomachache better than anyone. She's also terrific at "urping." After her third fake-heave, the school nurse sends her home for the day.

oOOoh!! I think I have the bubonic plague! I'm sure I'll feel better tomorrow....

My limo picks her up at her house. Ms. Warkentien shows us both how to make clouds in a measuring cup with ice cubes and hot water (apparently, we might have a two-minute science fair on the ride to work tomorrow), and then Gilda hangs with me in my dressing room while we wait for rehearsal to start. We spend the time brainstorming bits for her short film. After we have everything more or less blocked out, she picks up the script for *Jamie Funnie*.

"You want to run your lines?" she asks.

"I guess we'd better..."

And that's when Donna Dinkle, in full Jillda costume and makeup, swoops into the room. She has some sort of newspaper hidden behind her back.

"I hope I'm not interrupting anything important," she says, fluttering her eyelashes.

Talk about weird. It's like I'm seeing double. Gilda and Jillda.

"Jamie," says Donna, very dramatically, "I want to apologize for making that nasty remark after you choked and froze and totally looked like a stuffed deer with marble eyeballs."

I sort of nod. "Thanks. I think."

"The next time he freezes," cracks Gilda, "he knows how to turn it into a cloud."

Donna ignores her. "I only said those nasty words, Jamie, because I care. Maybe I care too much."

Gilda starts making *urp* noises again. "Sorry. Think I might barf."

Donna keeps going. "Jamie, I forgot that you were, you know, *otherwise abled*. Maybe choking like that is the best you can do, given your special needs."

Okay. She's really starting to work my last nerve. "What do you mean?"

"You know. You're crippled. Handicapped. Physically challenged."

"Stick a sock in it, sister," snaps Gilda.

"Why? Who are you?"

"Jamie's real friend."

Donna props her hand on her hip and glares at Gilda. "Well, when your 'friend' freezes, he isn't very funny."

"Did you catch him on *Saturday Night Live*?" says Gilda. "When he's working with the right people, he's hysterical."

Donna quivers her lip like she's about to burst into tears. "The right people? Was that a cut? Why do you have to be such a mean girl?"

"Why do you have to wear that Pirates hat?"

Donna gasps and covers her mouth with a trembling hand. Tears streak down her cheeks. I have a feeling she brought her onion chunks to work today.

"Look, Donna," I say, "I accept your apology. And I'm sorry if Gilda upset you."

"You should be," she says. "Because you need me, Jamie Grimm."

"Really?" Gilda laughs. "Why?"

"Because I know people who know people who know these people."

She slams her tabloid newspaper down on my makeup counter. It's open to Page Six.

The gossip column.

Or maybe we should call it my obituary.

Grimm's Future Looks Grim. Is the LIVE SHOW DEAD?

Headline writers excited about the puns-abilities.

Chapter 42

GOING VIRAL
CAN MAKE YOU SICK

It's sort of gone viral," says Donna. "Who knew my one itsy-bitsy little tweet about how unfunny you are would get retweeted, like, a bazillion times?"

 Jamie Grimm better not get 2 close 2 a pile of mashed potatoes next Thanksgiving. Prediction? Live show will be a turkey. #GrimmISaGONER

268 RETWEETS **753** FAVORITES

 Jamie Grimm's goose is cooked. #GrimmISaGONER
27 RETWEETS **68** FAVORITES

 Kid Comic is toast. #GrimmISaGONER
124 RETWEETS **53** FAVORITES

 These Jamie Grimm tweets are making me hungry. #turkeyontoast
17 RETWEETS **21** FAVORITES

"By the way," Donna continues, "Biff Bilgewater from *Hollywood Tonight* is running a piece tonight about how sad it is that no one will ever see my magnificent performance in this show. Biff's a CPF."

"An accountant?" says Gilda.

"No, Miss Clueless. A close personal friend. Ciao for now. Great meeting you, Hilda."

Donna sashays out of the dressing room.

Gilda and I both check our phones.

Donna wasn't lying. The rumors are flying. It's everywhere. Facebook. TMZ. People.com. Washed-up-people.com. There are even video clips of me staring blankly at the camera from last Friday.

It's amazing how much this kid sweats when he freezes. At the very least, he has a bright future working as a lawn sprinkler.

#GRIMMisAgoner

"How'd they get that footage?" I mumble.

"Two guesses," says Gilda, narrowing her eyes. "And they both should be Donna Dinkle."

"*Jamie Funnie?*" Biff says in the video clip. "*Not according to my inside sources. Yes, he was amusing in his brief guest shot on* SNL *because he was working with a true pro, Jacky Hart. But his own show? Sources tell me things look grim for young Jamie Grimm. Grim as in dismal, gloomy, abominable, atrocious, appalling…*"

We thumb him off the screen and check out a few more of the one hundred and sixty-seven thousand results to our Google search of the key words *Jamie Grimm stinks*.

The general consensus seems to be that I'm not really funny. That I just got lucky when I won the Planet's Funniest Kid Comic Contest. That Jacky Hart, Tina Fey, and Charlie Garner made me "seem funny" on *Saturday Night Live*. Rumors are flying that the BNC network is either going to postpone or completely cancel the show before it even goes on the air.

"Well," says Gilda, "looks like you've got something to prove again."

She's right.

Ever since the accident, a lot of people have made the mistake of underestimating me, the way they underestimate everyone in a wheelchair. Just because we can't use our legs, they think we can't do anything else, either.

Time to show them they're wrong.

Again.

Chapter 43

THE LONG RIDE TO NOWHERESVILLE

I roll into rehearsal and I don't choke or freeze or bomb.

I'm actually pretty good, if I say so myself.

So, the next morning, knowing there's only four more days before the big live broadcast on Friday night, I'm raring to go. The more we rehearse, the more confident I feel.

I roll out the door bright and early.

The limo isn't there. Neither is my tutor, Ms. Warkentien.

Instead, BNC has sent an Access-A-Ride handicapped taxi and a driver named Fred.

Guess there've been some budget cuts on *Jamie Funnie*.

While Fred is hoisting me up on the hydraulic chairlift, Gilda, Gaynor, and Pierce come running up the sidewalk.

"Jamie!" shouts Gilda. "Wait! This is super-important!" She's waving a sheet of paper.

"Um, can we wait a second, Fred?"

The driver shrugs. "Whatever. My meter's running." He ambles over to the driver's seat, leaving me suspended halfway between the sidewalk and the van.

"Where's the limo, dude?" asks Gaynor, eye-balling my humble handicapped van.

"This is no way to treat a TV star," adds Pierce.

"So, uh, what's so super-important?" I ask Gilda, basically ignoring Gaynor and Pierce.

"I just found out there's a deadline. For my film. Okay, I could've found out, like, last week, but I forgot to read the fine print on the e-mail...."

Fine print? I can relate.

"I have to send in my finished movie *in two days!* That means we have to shoot this afternoon so I have at least a day to put it all together."

"We've scheduled the filming for four o'clock," says Pierce. "On the boardwalk."

"Cool," I say.

Pierce checks his notebook, where I see he has drawn up some kind of scheduling flowchart. "You typically wrap your rehearsals around three, so you have an hour for the commute from Queens."

"You can even get there around four thirty," says Gilda. "We'll have to set up the cameras and lights and stuff. Vincent will be getting into his bully costume and makeup around three."

"But," says Pierce, checking his chart, "we have

to be completely done in time to return all the camera gear to the rental facility by eight."

"So be there or be square," adds Gaynor. "Uncle Frankie taught me that. People used to say it in, like, the Civil War or something."

"But I can't say for sure they'll let me out at three," I tell my friends.

"Why not?" says Gilda. "You're the star. Hello? They can't do *Jamie Funnie* without a Jamie playing Jamie."

"But it's not that simple—"

"Then make it simple."

Finally, Fred the driver starts honking his horn.

"Hey, look at me," he shouts. "I'm a tooter now, just like you wanted. Can we leave already? I've got two more pickups at the old folks' home."

"Four o'clock, Jamie," Gilda pleads. "Otherwise, I don't have a movie. And if I don't have a movie, I won't have a college scholarship, either."

I nod.

I understand.

I also know that if I goof up again on *Jamie Funnie*, Uncle Frankie won't have a diner.

And I won't have a house.

HURRY UP AND WAIT

When I arrive at Silvercup Studios, Ms. Wilder, the producer, tells me to wait in my dressing room.

"Brad will call you when he's ready for you."

"Great," I say. "Thanks."

And then I sit in my dressing room and wait.

Then I wait some more.

I wait for a very long time.

Finally, around two o'clock in the afternoon, Ms. Wilder comes back to escort me to the set.

"Sorry to keep you waiting. Brad's been busy."

"Working out camera moves with Mr. Wetmore?"

"No," she says. "Holding auditions."

She slides open the door to Studio B. I do not like what I see. Because I'm not the only kid in a wheelchair with a 1970s haircut and a puffy vest.

"I'm taking out a little antifreeze insurance," the director says while I gawk at my sea of doppelgangers. "But don't worry. You'll get a shot, too."

I gulp. "A shot?"

"We're willing to let you audition for the role of Jamie," says Ms. Wilder. "We figure it's only fair. After all, you've come this far."

"B-b-but…I'm—"

"Take a seat, Jamie," says Brad Grody.

All the actors angling for my job snicker. Because I already have a seat.

Fuming inside, I find a parking spot near the front row of seats.

"Okay," says Mr. Grody, "who's up next?"

"Shecky," says Ms. Wilder. "He's from Schenectady."

A kid in a wig much too big for his head rolls forward. "And just so you guys know," he whines, wagging his finger at me, "I almost beat the Grimm-meister in the New York round of the funny kid competition."

I have my head in my hands.

I cannot believe this.

Shecky from Schenectady was one of the New York comics I defeated in the second round of the Planet's Funniest Kid Comic Contest. All he had in his routine were recycled Henny Youngman jokes. Like, "I know a man who's a diamond cutter. He mows the grass at Yankee Stadium."

Now he might play me? On national TV?

Oh, the horror. The horror.

Chapter 45

I'VE NEVER LIKED ME LESS

It's like looking in a mirror. One of those warped ones in a fun house.

My nightmare goes on for hours.

And hours.

I think they see every kid from Uncle Chuckles' Comedy Boot Camp, a school in New York City that trains young stand-up comedians. They audition kids who've been in Broadway musicals. They even give the pizza delivery guy a script and ask him to sit down and say a few lines.

Then they bring in a guy I met (and beat) at the regionals up in Boston: Little Willy Creme, the cousin of a pretty famous comedian named Billy Creme. Dressed in jeans, a white T-shirt, and a black leather jacket (just like Billy), Little Willy always delivers his jokes with a nasty edge, like he's slashing his audience with his razor-sharp 'tude.

I hunch down in my chair. If Little Willy knows I'm in his audience, he might turn on me the way some comics do when they trash hecklers or make fun of the people they can see in the front rows.

"Yeah, my school has these NO BULLYING ZONE posters all over the place," he says, doing my opening monologue.

Well, it *used* to be my opening monologue.

Suddenly Little Willy stops.

"Can I rewrite these lines?" he asks the director. "Because, not for nothin', they stink. Like cheese. The old moldy stuff French people eat."

"Sure, Willy. Just make us laugh."

"I'll try, but no promises. It's hard to be funny when the words aren't. Nothing personal, pal, but this script is lame. Almost as lame as Jamie Grimm."

O-kay. He saw me.

"Jamie Grimm is such a lousy stand-up comic, he can't even stand up."

"How about we stick a little closer to the monologue?" says Mr. Grody.

"I'm gettin' there, pal. Sheesh, give a guy some artistic freedom, why don't ya? Okay, my school has this stupid no-bullying zone. Some knucklehead vice principal hung up all sorts of ridiculously stupid signs in the hallway. NO BULLYING. READERS ARE LEADERS. You ask me, cheaters are leaders, because they always know the answer. Who cares how they got it? Another sign actually says EXIT, but they won't let me exit the building. If I do as the sign suggests and skip school, they'll send the truant officers after me. The cops, too. So why put up the stupid EXIT sign *if you can't exit?*"

He's practically spitting.

"And another thing: Why no bullies? Bullies are people, too. I've decided the best way to beat the bullies is to become one. You get in my way, I'll roll right over you. You ever seen a chariot race? I'll put spikes in my spokes."

This is beyond bad.

And then, just like always, it gets worse. The director turns to the producer after Willy Creme is finished demolishing my monologue. "When does Chatty Patty get here?" Grody asks.

"Tomorrow," says Ms. Wilder. "Midmorning."

"Who invited her?" demands Little Willy Creme.

"Joe Amodio."

"Why? He's already got me."

"But Chatty Patty Dombrowski made it all the way to the finals," Ms. Wilder says with a smile.

I muster all my courage, roll out of the shadows, and raise my hand. "What about me?"

Brad Grody smirks. "Tell you what, Jamie—why don't you take tomorrow off? I want to work with Miss Dombrowski, Shecky from Schenectady, and Little Willy Creme. The rest of you can go home. Thanks for coming in."

Shecky and Willy do triumphant arm pumps. "Booyah!"

The other Jamie wannabes climb out of their

wheelchairs and, dejected, walk toward the exits.

"I'm happy to come in and work with you tomorrow, too," I tell Grody.

"That's okay, Jamie. I already know what you can do."

"Yeah," says Donna from her perch behind Mr. Grody's director's chair. "We *all* know what you can do: freeze the second the camera comes on."

There's nothing left for me to do but head for home.

I roll out of the soundstage and into the lobby.

A giant TV mounted on the wall is tuned to BNC. A promo fills the screen.

I whip my head around to check out the clock.

It's eight!

Even if we lived in Central time, I'm three hours late for Gilda's shoot on the boardwalk.

Here on the East Coast, it's more like *four!*

Chapter 46

WORLD'S WORST FRIEND? ME

The Access-A-Ride driver, of course, is late picking me up.

"Sorry, kid. It was bingo night at the senior center."

I ask him to drop me off at the boardwalk. But it's nearly ten PM by the time we reach Long Beach.

So I ask him to drop me off at Gilda's house.

I text her to let her know I'm coming.

When we pull into the driveway, all my friends are waiting for me on the front lawn.

Pierce speaks first. "As we told you, Jamie, we had to return the rented equipment by eight o'clock."

"That was, like, a couple hours ago," adds Gaynor.

"It was *like* a couple hours ago because it *was* a couple hours ago!" says Gilda.

I can tell she's steamed.

"Look, you guys, I'm sorry. It was a bad day."

Gilda gives me a look. It's not a nice one. "Welcome to the club."

"Despite your absence," says Vincent optimistically, "I think we came up with some pretty nifty material. See, I played you, Jamie, only we didn't do it in a wheelchair."

"I was the bully," says Gaynor. "I wasn't really mean, because I'm too chill."

"So I had to run the camera," says Pierce. "I used my other hand to hold the lights."

222

"Because I had to be in the scene," says Gilda. "Remember? It was a movie about directing a movie. Or have you completely forgotten your own lousy idea for an even lousier short film?"

"I am so, so sorry," I say.

You know that second-worst night of my life I told you about? Forget it. We have a new champion. *This* night.

"What can I do to make it up to you?" I ask. "Can I talk to the film-contest people and ask for an extension?"

"Look, Jamie," says Gaynor, "we totally get it. Your sitcom dealio is the most important thing in the universe. But other people have universes with super-important dealios in them, too."

"Well," says Vincent, "I, for one, think the final film will be terrific!"

"No, Vincent," says Gilda, sounding dejected. "I scrolled through the takes. It's bad. Plus, the judges only let me jump to the finals because I promised them that my 'good friend,' the big-shot TV star Jamie Grimm, would be the star of my short. Ask me how well that worked out."

No one says a word.

"Good night, you guys," says Gilda, sounding exhausted. "I need to go to bed."

She slumps her shoulders and sort of trudges up the walkway to her front door. Gaynor heads right, Pierce heads left.

"Well," says Vincent, "guess I better make like a banana and split."

Even he walks away.

I want to run after them. To promise I'll make it up to them. To tell Gilda that I haven't ruined her chance for a scholarship to her dream school.

But I can't do anything.

I can't run, I can't walk, I can't even play myself in a sitcom about my own life.

Yep. This is definitely the second-worst night of my life.

Chapter 47

IT'S ALWAYS DARKEST
BEFORE IT GETS DARKER

I start the long and lonely trek home to Smileyville.

It's so late, nobody else is on the streets of Long Beach. I have the road to myself. The potholes, too.

I'm alone with my thoughts.

How did I get myself into this mess?

Why did I ever want to be famous?

Wait a second. Fame was never really my goal. I just wanted to laugh. To wipe away some of the pain that came from remembering what happened that horrible night on the rain-slicked highway.

The truck. The car crash. Losing my parents *and* my baby sister.

I figured if I could learn to laugh after that, maybe I could help other people laugh their way through hard times, too. Laughter is the best medicine. Until it isn't anymore. Then you're, more or less, left with tears. Even if you use baby shampoo.

Trust me. I tried. It didn't work.

When I'm home and safely locked inside my garage bedroom, my phone starts ringing.

It's Donna Dinkle.

"Hiya, Jamie. So, did you hear the news? You're off the show. They're going to give that girl from Minnesota an audition tomorrow morning, but they've pretty much decided that Little Willy Creme should play you. He got my vote, too. He's a good kisser. Have a great night. And, Jamie?"

I'm so bummed, all I can manage is a very weak "Yeah?"

"Choose your friends more carefully next time. Pick people who can help you get where you want to go. I made the same mistake you made right before Fox canceled *Ring My Bell*. But, trust me, I'll never make it again. Ciao for now."

I'm glad when she hangs up. I've definitely heard enough.

I'm off the show.

I'm not Jamie Funnie anymore.

I also owe Joe Amodio one million dollars. What am I going to tell Uncle Frankie? Maybe I could carry a tub of hot dogs in my lap and hold an umbrella, and together we could open up our own rolling food cart.

My phone rings again.

"Jamie? Rose Skye Wilder from Joe Amodio Productions. We've cleaned out your dressing room, but you need to turn in your costume."

"What costume?"

"The sweater-vest. They tell me you wore it home?"

"This is *my* sweater-vest!"

"Really? Looks just like the one our main character always wears."

"Because I *am* the main character!"

"Not anymore. We need it back. Little Willy ripped the head hole in his. Buh-bye."

She hangs up.

Feeling lower than low, I know I can't go to sleep. I wheel myself out to the boardwalk.

Even though it's past midnight, Cool Girl

is there, just like I hoped she would be.

"How come you always know when I'm going to need to talk to you?" I ask.

She shrugs. "I might have a sixth sense. Or I might just read the gossip blogs."

She shows me the screen of her phone. According to the headlines, I've reached my "Grimm End."

"That's the problem with a name like mine," I say with a sigh. "It's so easy to make puns out of it. Tomorrow they'll probably say Grimm's fairy tale doesn't have a happy ending."

"So, they're hiring someone else to play you?" says Cool Girl.

"Yes. A meaner, nastier version of me."

"Mean and nasty isn't you, Jamie."

"I hope not."

"It isn't," says Cool Girl. "Your heart is too big to ever be that small."

And then guess what?

She doesn't kiss me. Again.

(I really thought she might this time.)

Chapter 48

GOOD NEWS/BAD NEWS

If there's an upside to being fired from my own sitcom, it's that I have all the time in the world to go to that library lunch sponsored by the Books of Hope charity.

Of course, there's also a downside: I have to explain to Uncle Frankie why I'm totally free for the day.

I've got good news and bad news. The good news is I have nothing on my schedule for the rest of the week. The bad news is I have nothing on my schedule for the rest of the week.

"They did the impossible," I tell him when we're in his van the next day, on our way to the library gig. "They replaced me. *Jamie Funnie* is being done without Jamie Grimm."

"No way."

"Way."

"We should go straight to the BNC headquarters building in Manhattan," says Uncle Frankie. "Threaten them with all sorts of bad publicity!"

"Can we just go entertain the kids at the library instead?"

Uncle Frankie glances over at me and smiles. "Sure thing, kiddo."

Suddenly, my phone starts chirping.

It's Mr. Wetmore, the technical director on the *Jamie Funnie* show.

"Hey, Jamie. Hope I didn't catch you at a bad time."

"No, sir. We're on our way to the Long Beach Public Library to entertain some really cool kids."

"Sounds like fun, but you need to come back to Silvercup Studios today. Three o'clock sharp."

"Why? Does Ms. Wilder still want my sweater-vest? Because I told her yesterday, it's not a costume, it's just what I wear, even though nobody else has worn a puffy vest since, like, 1986."

Mr. Wetmore laughs. "No, Jamie. This has nothing to do with your wardrobe. It's an audition."

"For what?"

"For you. Jacky Hart and I made a few calls. Mr. Amodio is willing to give you another chance."

"Seriously?"

"I told him my own daughter wouldn't watch the show if you weren't in it. Jacky told him you're made for live TV. You're on at three, Jamie."

"We'll be there!"

"What's up?" asks Uncle Frankie when I thumb off my phone.

"Do you believe in miracles?" I say.

"Hey, I'm looking at you, aren't I?" Then he reaches over and tousles my hair.

I love when he does that.

"Mr. Wetmore arranged an audition for me. For *Jamie Funnie*!"

"Excellent," says Uncle Frankie. "For what part?"

"I'm not sure. Maybe Jillda Jewel."

Uncle Frankie is cracking up. "Come on. Let's go warm up your funny bones!"

We pull into the library parking lot and roll up the handicapped ramp.

It's showtime.

Chapter 49

SHHH! IT'S A LIBRARY!

The kids all shriek when I roll into the library.

Yep, they treat me like a rock star. And I have to say, it feels fantastic to hear that applause again.

Being funny should be fun.

Right now, it is.

"Hi, guys," I say, popping a few wheelies. "I'm Jamie Grimm, and it's great to be here. Anybody read a good book recently?"

The kids all scream, "I did, I did!"

"My Uncle Frankie is going to show you a few yo-yo tricks later on. And guess what? He learned every single one of them from a book."

"It's true," Uncle Frankie chimes in.

"In fact," I say, "if Uncle Frankie couldn't read, he'd probably think his yo-yo was a very quiet plastic pet on an extremely short leash."

I mime Uncle Frankie tugging on a string, talking to a yo-yo on the floor.

"'That's a good boy. Play dead. Roll over. Okay, keep playing dead.' Trust me, you guys—reading is super-important. You can't do anything or go anywhere without reading. I said the same thing to my cousin Stevie the other day, and he said, 'Oh, really? I don't need to read in the bathroom.' And I said, 'When you're in the shower, how do you know which bottle is the shampoo and which one is the toilet-bowl cleaner? Or is that why you have that bald spot?'"

While the kids are laughing, I check out the crowd. Cool Girl is in the house.

I see her smiling in the back of the room. A happy girl, maybe six years old, is sitting on her lap holding a picture book.

"I like reading so much," I say, "I just started studying speed-reading. Last night, I read *Harry Potter* in five seconds! I know it's only two words, but, hey, it's a start."

Another wave of laughter washes over me, and I feel a surge of happiness I haven't felt in way too long.

This is why I love comedy.

Not for the fame or the glory or even the million-dollar checks that aren't really worth a million bucks.

I love comedy because laughing makes me feel good. It makes me glad to be alive.

After my set, Uncle Frankie wows the crowd with all the tricks he learned from those yo-yo books.

The kids give him a standing ovation. I would've too, but, well…you know.

Shortest book in the library? Well, there are a few. <u>The Fat, Lard, and Cream Diet</u>. <u>Everything Boys Know About Girls</u>. And my favorite, <u>Different Ways to Spell "Bob."</u>

When we're all done and busy signing autographs for our adoring fans, Cool Girl comes up to me.

"So, Jamie," she says, coolly of course. "Do you remember who you are?"

"Yep," I say with a grin. "I funny."

And guess what?

This time she *does* kiss me!

Chapter 50

TIME FLIES WHEN YOU'RE HAVING FUN

I'm having so much fun being funny, I sort of lose track of time.

Good thing Uncle Frankie doesn't.

"Come on, Jamie. We need to get you over to the studio, pronto!"

I'm thinking about lingering at the library. Okay, I'm thinking about that kiss from Cool Girl. Wondering if there might be a second one coming my way.

But Uncle Frankie's right. We need to roll!

Fortunately, for once, the Long Island Expressway isn't a parking lot. We make it to Silvercup Studios in the nick of time.

Or, judging by the posters we see in the lobby, we might be too late.

"You're here," says Mr. Wetmore when he sees us in the lobby. "Good. We'll be uplinking your audition to LA. Joe Amodio came in from the golf course to see Little Willy Creme and you, Jamie."

"How was Little Willy?" asks Uncle Frankie.

"Nasty, foul, and angry."

"Was he funny?" I ask timidly.

"A couple guys in the control booth laughed, but not me."

"What about Mr. Amodio?" I ask.

Mr. Wetmore puts his hand on my shoulder. "Jamie? Can I give you a little advice?"

"Sure."

"Don't worry about Mr. Amodio. Just be you."

Uncle Frankie puts his hand on my other shoulder.

"I agree," he says. "You funny."

And so, at exactly 2:59 PM, I roll back onto the comedy club set.

The director, Brad Grody, is sitting in the audience. So are Little Willy Creme, Donna Dinkle, Stewart Johnson, Ms. Wilder, and all those other people in suits.

But you know what? I don't really see them.

I see Cool Girl, telling me I have a big heart.

I see the kids at the library, laughing when I popped a wheelie.

I see those elementary schoolers who love telling me jokes just because it's fun to crack each other up.

That's who I want to be. One of those kids.

I want to laugh just because I'm extremely happy that I still can.

So, I get going.

"Hi, I'm Jamie Grimm. It's great to be back. Y'know, my school has these NO BULLYING ZONE posters hanging all over the place. Only one problem: Bullies aren't big readers. Reading's not really a job requirement in the glamorous field of wedgie yanking."

I nail the opening monologue. People are laughing.

Then I veer off script and improvise a little.

"It's true. Bullies don't read. Not even in the bathroom. I guess that might explain why the biggest bully at my middle school, Lars from Mars, brushes his teeth with pimple cream. Read the label, Lars. Oh, right. You don't like to read. Guess that's why, every morning, you spray your armpits with a can of Cheez Whiz."

What can I say? I'm having a blast.

In fact, I'm having so much fun, I don't even care if I get the part.

Chapter 51

ON A ROLL

I do, like, fifteen minutes of material. Some from the script. Some straight off the top of my head.

When I'm done, even Little Willy Creme concedes defeat.

"You do the whole wheelchair schtick way better than me, man," he says.

Donna Dinkle, who, by the way, might be the biggest phony I've ever met in my life, runs over and actually hugs me—chair and all.

"Okay, let him breathe," says Uncle Frankie, gently pushing Donna aside. "Whoo, is there a Cinnabon near here?"

"No," I say with a grin. "It's her perfume."

"Huh. Thought I was at the mall…"

We're both laughing when Brad Grody saunters over.

"Little dude, this is totes awk. Sorry. It just didn't do it for me. I'm not feeling the funny."

"You know what, fur face?" snarls Little Willy Creme. "Maybe you should go back to lumberjack school or wherever you picked up that flannel shirt."

"Easy, Willy. You're my pick for the part."

Willy does this sort of sideways sneer. "Well, big

dude, you're totes wrong. Only Jamie was born to play this role."

"Actually," I say, "I wasn't born to play it. I sort of grew into it."

Mr. Grody turns to one of his assistants. "Is Chatty Patty still in the building? I'd like Mr. Amodio to hear her do the part, as well."

"I'd like to audition, too," says Donna Dinkle, batting her eyelashes at the director. "I know how to drive a wheelchair."

"No need, Donna," says Mr. Wetmore, striding onto the set, holding out his phone. "Joe's heard enough. He wants to talk to Jamie."

Uh-oh. This is it.

The final heave-ho.

Mr. Amodio is giving my part to Little Willy.

I'm about to go into my standard panic mode and start spritzing sweat when Mr. Wetmore gives me a wink.

Well, what do you know?

I believe Mr. Wetmore already had a private chat with Mr. Amodio.

I also believe Uncle Frankie will be keeping his diner. And Smileyville will still be Smileyville!

"We go out live Friday night," says Mr. Amodio. "The day after tomorrow. If you need anything, anything at all…"

"Well, sir, actually, I do need something." My voice only cracks twice. It also squeaks a little.

"Name it, kiddo. You've got it."

I take a deep breath and close my eyes. Summon up every ounce of courage I can find. "I need a new director."

Brad Grody gasps. "Why, I never…"

"Yeah, well, get used to it," cracks Little Willy. "I have a feeling it's gonna happen to you a lot, pal, because, face it: You're a lousy director."

While Little Willy keeps blasting Brad Grody with insults, I plead my case with Mr. Amodio.

"We need a fresh pair of eyes, Mr. Amodio. Someone who really knows how to work with actors."

"It's a little late to change horses, Jamie baby. We're kind of in midstream here."

"We need Gilda Gold."

"Gilda who?"

"Gold. She directed the short film that got me to the semifinals in Las Vegas."

"That comedy concert in the school corridor? I saw that on YouTube. I *loved* that video. It was terrific."

"Well, sir, Gilda's the one who made it that way. She was my director."

"Is that so? Is she available?"

I smile. "Yes, sir. I'm pretty sure she is."

"Then it's settled. Put me on speakerphone. Brad?"

The director shoots me a dirty look. "What?"

"You're fired. And Jamie, go get me this Gilda Gold. She's our new director."

Wow! This is great. Gilda's going to direct me in a live TV show.

I just hope she's willing to listen to me so I can tell her.

Chapter 52

BUH-BYE, BRAD

Brad Grody storms off the set in a huff.

Good luck, Lamie Jamie. You're gonna need it.

Maybe. But I definitely don't need *you*.

"Good riddance to bad rubbish," says Uncle Frankie.

"Hear, hear," adds Nigel Bigglebottom, the British actor playing Uncle Frankie in the show. "Bit of a dolt, eh, what?"

"Does 'dolt' mean he's an idiot?" asks Uncle Frankie.

"Indeed."

"Then I agree. Biggest dolt I ever met."

"I am *soooo* glad we're getting a new director," says Donna Dinkle, batting her eyelashes at me this time. "Sure, we only have, like, less than two days to make any changes he might suggest…"

"It's a *she*," I remind her. "Gilda Gold. Your part, Jillda Jewel, is based on her."

"Really? Super. Can't wait to meet her."

I would tell Donna that she already met Gilda, but I'd probably be wasting my breath. So instead, I simply say, "You might ask wardrobe to find you a Boston Red Sox cap."

"Why?"

"It's Gilda's favorite team."

Her eyes widen with delight. "Thanks for the tip, JG!" She dashes off to talk with (or scream at) the costumers.

251

"Do you have Ms. Gold's phone number?" asks Mr. Wetmore.

I nod.

"Guess we better call her. See if she's up for the job."

"Yeah."

And now I start sweating.

What if Gilda is still steamed at me? What if she refuses to direct my show because she can't stand being in the same room (or television studio) with me? What if she treats me the way I sort of treated her?

"You okay?" asks Mr. Wetmore.

I gulp. "Never better."

"You look kind of queasy," says Uncle Frankie.

"Bad shrimp salad for lunch. It tasted a little off."

"Jamie? You had soup for lunch."

"See? I told you that shrimp tasted funny."

"Are you stalling?" he asks.

"Totally."

Uncle Frankie puts a gentle hand on my shoulder. "Gilda's a good friend, Jamie. She might bust your chops a little, but don't worry—in the end, she'll always be on your side."

I hope he's right. I make the call. To my relief, she answers.

"Gilda? It's me. Jamie."

"Who?" she says, pretending not to recognize my voice.

"Jamie Grimm."

"Oh, right. I had a friend named Jamie Grimm once. Nice kid. If you ever bump into him, tell him I miss him."

"I miss you, Gilda," I tell her. "That's why I want to work with you."

"On what? All the homework you skipped while you were off being a TV star?"

"No. I need your help on my TV show."

There is a long pause.

"You know—*Jamie Funnie*."

An even longer pause.

So I start rambling. "We just fired the director and the show goes on the air live the day after tomorrow and I told Joe Amodio, he's the producer, that you would be the best person to take over for Brad Grody, who, as his name implies, is totally grody and kept trying to replace me and then… hang on."

Mr. Wetmore is gesturing for me to hand him my phone.

"Ms. Gold?" he says. "This is Richard Wetmore, tech director on Jamie's show. He'd like you to take over for Mr. Grody. Jamie says you're the best director he's ever worked with, and our producer, Joe Amodio, loved what you did with Jamie's hallway comedy concert on YouTube. Of course, you'll have to miss school tomorrow and

Friday. Great. We'll send a limo to pick you and Jamie up first thing in the morning. Right. See you tomorrow."

Mr. Wetmore hands me back my phone.

"She's in?" I ask.

"Yep."

"Guess I should've mentioned that get-out-of-school-free stuff to her earlier, huh?"

"Yep."

"Good to know."

Donna Dinkle races back onto the set. She's wearing a BoSox baseball cap and a new wig. In fact, her Jillda now looks exactly like Gilda.

"How's this, Jamie?" she gushes.

"Perfect. But, Donna?"

"Yes?"

"Gilda Gold is going to be our director. That means we both have to listen to her and do what she tells us to do."

Donna giggles. "I know that, silly goose. Don't forget, I've been a TV star my whole life. Now, if you guys will excuse me, I need to tell wardrobe to bedazzle this baseball cap. Add some sequins and shiny baubles."

"B-b-but…"

She's gone before I can suggest that she wait to see what Gilda thinks of her costume.

Uncle Frankie taps me on the shoulder.

"You need to keep an eye on that one," he says. "She looks like trouble."

I agree. Trouble with a big, bedazzled *T*.

GILDA IN CHARGE

"This script is pretty good," says Gilda, flipping through the pages. "I'm not crazy about this scene. It's kind of flat."

"We can fix it. Mr. Amodio said he'd give us whatever we need."

"What about all the camera moves and sound cues?"

"Mr. Wetmore will handle those. You just make sure the actors are doing their jobs. Tell 'em it's your way or the highway."

"You're one of the actors, right?"

"It was a close call, but yep."

Gilda rubs her hands together gleefully. "Oh, this is going to be fun. Hey, do you think your new friend Jacky Hart might help us out?"

"Maybe. What's on your mind?"

"An idea for a surprise-guest-star appearance."

"By Jacky?

"And one of her *SNL* friends."

"I'll give her a call."

"You have Jacky Hart's phone number?"

"Office *and* cell."

"Wow. I'm impressed."

I shrug. "It's no biggie. Both her daughters are big fans of mine."

"Well, that makes three of us."

All of a sudden, I have this lump the size of a meatball in my throat. "You're still a fan?"

"Always have been, Jamie. Always will be. Besides, it's kind of hard to stay mad at a guy who gives you the biggest break of your life!"

She leans over and gives me a quick peck on the cheek. Under the circumstances, I might like Gilda's kiss even more than Cool Girl's!

As soon as we arrive at Silvercup Studios, Gilda jumps right in.

First, she works with me and the Frownie family on a scene where we're posing for our family Christmas card portrait.

259

"Hold those frowns, guys," Gilda coaches. "And if the audience laughs, try to look even more confused."

She turns to the animal trainer.

"Can you have the cat slump to the floor and cover its eyes with its paws?"

"We'll try," says the trainer. "But it's a cat."

Somehow, the guy makes it work. Watching the cat slump to the floor in sync with the Frownies' frowns? Hysterical.

Next, Gilda tackles the scene with me and Nigel Bigglebottom in the diner. She makes it much better.

Next up is my first scene with Donna Dinkle as Jillda Jewel. She meets me in homeroom, where I tell her all about the zombies I passed on my way to school.

"You know," I say, "zombies only date super-intelligent girls."

Donna bats her eyelashes. "I know. Because they love a girl with *braaaaains!*"

"Cut," says Gilda.

"Is there some problem?" asks Donna.

"Um, yeah. According to my script, you were supposed to say, 'Is that so?' and then Jamie does the line about 'braaaaains,' because the show's called *Jamie Funnie*, not *Jillda Funnie*."

Donna smiles and blinks. A lot.

"Ensemble shows work best when everybody shares the laugh lines," she says.

"Maybe," mumbles Gilda. I can see her wheels spinning. "Mr. Wetmore?" she says to the ceiling.

An intercom mic from the control booth clicks on. "What's up, Ms. Gold?"

"Is it too late to cast a few more characters? Extras?"

"Zombies?"

"You read my mind. This scene is kind of boring. Instead of Jamie *telling* Jillda about the zombies, it would be awesome if we *showed* them. Could we do some bloody costumes and gross makeup and play the scene in front of a scrolling backdrop—something simple to make it look like Jamie's rolling down the street and bumping into all sorts of weird zombies?"

"We could do it in front of the green screen," says Mr. Wetmore, "and add the rolling background with a video we run through the switcher."

"Awesome!"

"Let me make a few quick calls and get back to you."

"Thank you, Mr. Wetmore. And see if Jacky Hart will play one, too! Jamie has her phone numbers."

"Great idea."

"And we could have that lizard guy from *SNL* just sort of randomly lurching down the street. Like he's still bitter about losing to Jamie last weekend."

The whole crew is chuckling. They like Gilda's ideas.

Everybody on the set is happy. Except, of course, Donna Dinkle. She's seriously *un*happy.

"Am I in the scene?" she asks. "On the moving sidewalk?"

Gilda shakes her head. "No. It'd be too confusing. We'll introduce you later, in the cafeteria scene. That's where Jamie and I first met, anyway. Remember?"

I smile.

How could I forget? It's not every day you meet someone who loves comedy and making people laugh as much as you do.

Plus, she let me finish her chocolate milk.

Chapter 54

ALL MY SHIRTS ARE SWEATSHIRTS

Early Friday morning, I'm on BNC's *Sunrise Show* promoting that night's live broadcast.

Speaking of nerves, when I get to Silvercup Studios, Michael McKee, the actor playing my best friend, Bob, is waiting for me in my dressing room.

"Jamie?"

"Yes, Michael?"

"I have a confession to make."

"What? Are you the one who stole my M&M's?"

"No. That was Donna. She swiped my Twizzlers, too. I need to tell you that, well, sometimes I choke like you did."

"You do?"

"Not all the time. Just sometimes. Like when there's an audience or I'm doing a show live. I'm better working on movies. Or still photos. I'm fine on fashion shoots."

"Too bad our show is live and in front of an audience, then. You haven't choked in rehearsals, though."

"Only because you choked before I had a chance to go on and choke myself."

"Hey, you know what Jacky Hart told me when I did *SNL* last weekend?"

Michael shakes his head.

"There are no mistakes. They're just chances to do something even funnier."

"That's right," says a woman out in the hall.

Michael gasps. Because Jacky Hart just poked her head into my dressing room.

"Which way to wardrobe and makeup?" Jacky asks.

"Down the hall. Third door on your left."

"Thanks."

"No, thank *you*," I say. "It's so amazing that you're doing a guest shot on my first show!"

"Hey, it's Friday. I only work on Saturday nights.

Besides, I've always wanted to be a zombie."

She sticks out her arms Frankenstein-style and staggers down the hall. "Braaaaains. Must eat braaaaains. Or kidneys. Kidneys would be fine… just not kidney beans."

"Wow," says Michael when she's gone. "I can't believe you know Jacky Hart."

"I only met her last week. She's pretty awesome. You know, she told me she used to get so nervous in front of people that she'd stutter."

"Really? You'd never know it looking at her now."

"Exactly. And no one has to know that you and I wig out in front of a crowd, either. We just have to channel all that nervous energy into our performances."

"Did Jacky Hart tell you that, too?"

"No. That I got from Gilda Gold, our new director."

Suddenly, I hear a big, booming voice out on the set. "You're a *kid?!*"

It's Joe Amodio. I recognize his boom.

"You say that as if it's a bad thing."

That's Gilda. I think my producer just met my new director.

Chapter 55

CAUTION: CHILDREN AT PLAY

I wheel myself out to the set as fast as I can. Donna Dinkle is smirking as I fly by.

"I always said TV was run by a bunch of children, but this is ridiculous!" Mr. Amodio is shouting. Rose Skye Wilder winces and moves away from earsplitting range.

"She's doing a fantastic job, Joe," says Mr. Wetmore, leaping to Gilda's defense. "The fact that she's young just makes her that much more of a genius."

"Yeah," I say, sticking up for my friend. "What he said. Gilda's a genius."

Gilda blushes. "You really think so, Jamie?"

"Of course I do."

"B-b-but..." Mr. Amodio is sputtering. "My money...my millions..."

"My money is on the two kids," says Jacky Hart, coming onstage with a fake zombie arm dangling out of her shirt.

"What happened to your arm?"

She shrugs. "Fell off. And pretty soon, I won't have a leg to stand on."

"Welcome to the club," I crack.

"Joe, I'm Jacky Hart."

"I know who you are, Ms. Hart. I love you on *SNL*! And you're absolutely fantastic in that movie *Cracking Up*. I'm hearing Oscar buzz."

"Maybe you should see an ear doctor about that."

Mr. Amodio has stopped sputtering and is finally smiling.

"You know, Joe," Jacky says, "I took on a lot when I was Gilda's age. Someday I'll write a book about it."

"She's just a kid."

"And she's the best director you've got, not to mention the only one. Now, we have a show to prep."

"We sure do!" Mr. Amodio claps Gilda on the back and starts making a little speech to the cast and crew. "Welcome aboard, kiddo. I am so proud to be associated with *Jamie Funnie*. With Gilda here at the helm and Jamie in the starring role, not to

mention all the other kids in the cast, this show is
going to make TV history. Either that or tank. I'm
hoping for history. How about you guys?"

Everyone cheers and gives Mr. Amodio's pep talk
a rousing ovation.

Except Donna Dinkle.

She's kind of lurking off to the side, flapping her
arms like they're stubby wings, and making "gobble-
gobble" turkey sounds that no one hears but me.

Oh, yeah. She's definitely looking for this show to
tank. Big-time.

Chapter 56

MAKE ROOM FOR ZOMBIES!

The clock is ticking.

We have time for one last rehearsal before they start letting the studio audience take their seats.

"Let's run the zombie bit," says Gilda. "Where's my space lizard?"

"Greetings, earthling," says Charlie Garner, the other *SNL* cast member, who'll be making a surprise appearance on my show. He's costumed just like he was on Saturday night.

"We save you for last," says Gilda.

"You got it, *bubelah*," says Garner, who's already in character.

"You sure you don't want me in this scene?" shouts Donna Dinkle from her perch in the cafeteria set. "I could make funny faces and pretend like the zombies are grossing me out. I do a great 'gag me now' gesture."

"We're better off saving you for the cafeteria scene," Gilda tells her. "We need to meet a fresh face in the second act."

"Because my face will have fallen off by then," cracks Jacky, who's in flesh-melting zombie makeup.

Every time we rehearse the scene, Jacky and her zombie friends ad-lib something even funnier than the last time we did it. I just sit there, pretending to work my arms as I fake-roll down the green screen "street," and let the gags fly. I have a couple, too.

"So, did you hear about the new zombie dating book?" I say to Jacky Hart.

She shakes her head, and her rubber nose flies off. "Sorry. Runny nose. What's the zombie dating book called?"

"Dying to Meet You!"

"Oh. That's a real knee-slapper. Wait, where's my knee? Did I slap it off?"

I point toward the floor. "It's in your shoe."

None of that was in the script. But it might be in the show! Because the crew is cracking up.

All of a sudden, I can't wait for it to be eight.

We retreat to our dressing rooms around seven.

The ushers open the doors for our studio audience at seven thirty. A lot of those kids in wheelchairs are back.

This time, I promise, I'll give them the kind of performance they deserve. One with words and, hopefully, lots of laughs.

Mr. Wetmore brings his daughter, Serena, backstage in her wheelchair to meet me. She has cerebral palsy, but that doesn't stop her from smiling the sunniest smile I've ever seen in my whole life.

"Jamie…you're my…favorite!"

It takes her a little time to get the words out, but I don't mind. When I look in her eyes, I can see all sorts of happiness. She makes me feel happy, too.

Chapter 57

GO TIME FOR SHOWTIME!

The stage manager, a lady named Gretchen who is wearing a head microphone like a football coach, comes into my dressing room.

"Jamie? Gilda's ready for you on set."

I wipe my hands on my pants to dry them off. "So this is it?"

"Yep," says Serena. "Break…a…leg, Jamie."

"No, thanks. Been there. Done that."

"It's a theater expression," says Mr. Wetmore. "'Break a leg' means 'Good luck.'"

"I know. But, with me, they really ought to change it to 'Blow a tire.'"

"Okay," says Serena. "Blow…a…tire, Jamie!"

Mr. Wetmore takes Serena, who's laughing so hard she's rocking in her wheelchair, back to her parking spot in the front row. I roll behind the scenery and make my way toward the comedy club backdrop, where I'll do my opening monologue.

As I cruise across the stage, all those kids in wheelchairs start applauding. Some even start up a "Jay-mee, Jay-mee!" chant. It's awesome.

Soon, the whole audience (except my fans in their wheelchairs) is on its feet and cheering. Uncle Frankie. The Smileys. Cool Girl and her parents. Gaynor and Pierce are standing right behind Gilda, who's standing right behind camera one.

I can't tell you how great it is to have my three best buds in the whole world so close on such a big night.

"We're live in five," says Gilda when I take my position behind the microphone stand in front of the brick wall of the comedy club set. "And, Jamie?"

"Yeah?"

"Remember: You funny!"

Gaynor and Pierce both shoot me double thumbs-ups.

I'm feeling pretty great. Running my lines in my head. Getting into the zone.

And then I see Stevie Kosgrov and Lars Johannsen.

The two delinquents are skulking around backstage, checking out all the electric cables they can yank out of plugs.

They're about to sabotage my show.

Chapter 58

BULLY STAMPEDE

A good director sees everything that happens on his or her set. Fortunately, Gilda is a *great* director.

She turns to Gretchen, the stage manager. "Alert security. Two goons stage right. Lose them."

"On it," says Gretchen. She touches her earpiece. Mumbles something.

Two seconds later, my big, burly bodyguards have Stevie and Lars cornered.

"We're just here to see the show," blubbers Stevie. "My cousin, the crip from Cornball, is the star."

"And Lars from Mars is supposed to be me!" shouts Lars.

"You boys can watch it out back," says one of the giant security guards. "We have a special TV set up there just for the two of you."

The guards escort the bullies out of the building.

I breathe a sigh of relief.

Which is a good thing. Because Gilda just said, "We're live in fifteen seconds."

The stage manager is pointing at me with all five fingers, ready to do her countdown.

The theme music and prerecorded opening credits fill every TV in the soundstage.

"Live from New York," booms an announcer, "it's *Jamie Funnie*, starring Jamie Grimm, the funniest kid comic on the planet. Also starring Donna Dinkle as Jillda Jewel. Tonight's special guest stars—direct from *Saturday Night Live*—Jacky Hart and Charlie Garner. Ladies and gentlemen, here he is, Jaaaaay-meeeeee Griiiiiiiimmmmmmmm!"

The stage manager points at me.

The red light on top of camera one blinks awake. I'm on.

Chapter 59

IF YOU'RE TALKING, YOU'RE NOT CHOKING

I smile and look straight into the camera lens.

I launch into my monologue. I do it exactly as scripted, until the end. "Bullies don't read. Not even in the bathroom. I guess that might explain why the biggest bully at my middle school, this incredible hulk everybody calls Lars from Mars, brushes his teeth with pimple cream. *Read the label, Lars.* Oh, right. You don't like to read. Every morning, you spray your armpits with a can of Cheez Whiz. No wonder you have that rodent problem in your locker."

I do a quick bucktoothed rat nibble.

"Nom, nom, nom."

Gilda's checking her script.

Because those last couple of lines aren't in it. She smiles.

And the audience is loving it.

The lights come up over on the Frownie family kitchen set. Mrs. Frownie is pretending to holler out the back door to me while I quickly roll over to the green screen to do the zombie bit.

"Jamie? Be careful on your way to school. The radio said today's a zombie alert day. And some of our neighbors only sleep when they're dead tired."

When I'm in front of the green screen, I fake like I'm pumping my wheels and talk directly to camera three.

"That's not what Mrs. Frownie really said. It's just what I heard. Because I have a very vivid imagination."

Extras playing flesh-dangling zombies start slouching past me.

"My neighbors are mostly sleepy-eyed commuters, shuffling off to work every morning like they're brain-dead. So to me, they look like zombies. Especially Mrs. Smith from next door."

Jacky Hart lumbers onstage. The audience gives her a round of entrance applause.

She waves at me. Her hand goes flying.

"Come on, kid," she says, "give me a hand. I just lost mine."

"So, um, what's your favorite street around here?" I ask her.

"The dead ends. Gotta go, kid. Pleased to eat you."

And that's when Charlie Garner, playing his space lizard, lurches down the street. "Hey, Jamie. I'm the funniest kid comic on my planet. I was robbed in that contest and I want a rematch. I challenge you to another battle of wits."

"Sorry," I say. "I never fight an unarmed alien."

Jacky shuffles back into the scene. This wasn't in the script. Yep, she's improvising. I notice that she's pulled her left arm out of her tattered shirt and that the sleeve is suddenly empty and flapping.

The applause light comes on. The audience claps like crazy. Theme music swells out of the speaker.

"And we're clear!" shouts Gilda. "Three-minute commercial break."

Gaynor and Pierce slap Gilda a high five.

I check out the kids in the wheelchairs down front. They're loving the show.

I check out the rest of the crowd, too. They're all smiling! *Everybody* loved the first two scenes.

Except, of course, Donna Dinkle. Because she wasn't in either one of them. She's over near the schoolyard set. Talking to Michael McKee.

And whatever she's telling him isn't doing much to calm Michael's nerves. In fact, my "best friend" Bob has a very familiar look in his eye. It's the one I always get right before I choke.

Chapter 60

SO FAR, SO GOOD!

Sixty seconds and we're back live," says Gretchen, the stage manager.

"Places for the schoolyard scene," says Gilda. "We need Jamie, Lars from Mars, and Bob."

Joe Amodio comes bounding onstage over to me. He's very, very happy.

"The network is tracking audience response at focus groups all across the country. You're scoring off the charts, kiddo. And they loved that bit with the zombies and then the lizard. Who came up with that?"

"Me and Gilda, I guess."

"Keep it up, you two. America loves what you're doing. Stay on a roll tonight, and we're definitely looking at a twenty-two episode commitment from BNC!"

"And Uncle Frankie gets to keep his diner?"

"Jamie, if you sign on for a full season, you can buy your uncle a whole string of diners."

"Thirty seconds," says Gretchen.

"Woo-hoo!" says Joe Amodio, as he, more or less, prances off the stage.

I roll over to the schoolyard set.

Michael McKee is standing near the edge. Trembling.

He looks totally freaked.

"Just relax," I tell him. "You'll be great as Bob."

"I'm Bob the Builder?"

"No…"

"SpongeBob SquarePants?"

Hoo-boy. Donna definitely did a number on the poor guy.

I can see her, smirking in the shadows behind camera three.

"Don't worry," I tell Michael. "Lars is on first. You have time to pull yourself together. Just breathe. Try to relax."

Michael nods. The way people who don't speak English do when they think you're asking them a question, but you're not.

"Five, four, three…"

The stage manager does the last two seconds of her countdown silently with her fingers. This is the problem with doing a live show. You can't stop when one of your cast mates turns into a frozen vegetable.

The red light comes on again.

The actor who plays Lars from Mars marches onto the set from stage left as I roll on from stage right. We meet in the middle as the transition music fades.

"Oh, hey, Lars," I say. "Flush any sixth graders down the toilet today?"

"Watch your mouth!"

"Why? Is it doing something weird?"

I scooch my lips around and make a bunch of funny faces. The audience is yukking it up.

Lars steps forward. "What, you think that just because you're in a wheelchair, I won't kick your butt into the next county?"

He puts his hands on his hips and scowls at me. You can see the steam shooting out of his ears—Gilda had the prop guys rig him up with crazy smoke-machine earpieces.

"You think you're so funny." Lars sneers. "Well, you know what they say about he who laughs last…"

"Um, he was too slow to get the joke the first time he heard it?"

"No! He who laughs last, laughs loudest!"

And then, just like he's supposed to, he shoves me. Hard.

I topple backward. Fortunately the whole "schoolyard" is actually a wrestling mat painted black and white to look like an asphalt basketball court. The mat cushions my fall.

Lars bends down to laugh in my face.

"Ha! Ha! Ha! I had the last laugh."

"Tee-hee. Did not."

Lars balls up his fist. "Ho, ho. Did too!"

He waits for me to dare to laugh again.

When I don't, he stomps offstage, leaving me stranded—just the way it actually happened when Stevie Kosgrov decked me on my first day at Long Beach Middle School.

But, back then, my friends raced to my rescue.

Which is what we have in the script, too. This is supposed to be my best friend Bob's big entrance.

"That'll teach you not to mess with me!" I call after Lars from Mars. Then—"Could you come back and help me up now?" I peep so pitifully the audience can't help but laugh.

I glance over at Bob.

Actually, I glance over to where Bob is supposed to be.

I'm all alone.

On live TV.

In front of millions of people.

Flat on my back.

Chapter 61

UNLESS I'M MISTAKEN,
THERE ARE NO MISTAKES

Okay. Time to improvise.

I can't put myself back in the wheelchair, which is lying on its side five feet away from me.

And Lars can't come back into the scene and help me out, because it would be totally out of character.

"Ha-ha." I say. "There. I had the last laugh. Ha. And the second-to-last laugh, too. Um, can somebody lend me a hand?"

Jacky Hart lurches back onstage in her zombie costume.

"Here you go, kid."

She tosses me a rubber hand.

The audience laughs. Jacky's trying to buy me

some time to think my way out of this mess.

"I'd love to help you out, Jamie," she says, "but I'm just a figment of your imagination."

"Right. Thanks for dropping by."

"No problem. I think I'll go inside and check out the teacher's lounge. I hear teachers have humongous brains…"

She exits.

The audience is still cracking up. They think this is all part of the bit. That's good.

"I think I broke my butt bone," I say, earning another laugh.

I turn my head sort of sideways.

"You ever have one of those days?" I say to the camera. "I do. All the time. Monday, Tuesday, Wednesday…"

I see Gilda next to the camera. Her hands are up. She doesn't know what to do. She raises her eyebrows and makes a slashing gesture across her throat.

Should I cut to a commercial? is what she's trying to ask me.

"But do I let it get me down?" I say. "Nope."

That's my way of telling Gilda to not call the cut. Everyone will know we messed up if she does.

I can't quit. Not in front of Serena Wetmore and all those other kids pulling for me. Just because we're in wheelchairs does not mean we're helpless. Sometimes, we just have to be a little more creative than everybody else.

I, once again, remember what Jacky Hart always says: *Every mistake is just a chance to do something even funnier.*

Like adding some characters to a live TV show who aren't even in the script!

"Yo, Gaynor? Pierce?" I shout. "A little help out here..."

While they look at each other and wonder what the heck I'm doing, I talk straight into that camera lens again.

"Joey Gaynor and Jimmy Pierce are the two best friends any guy could ever have. They never treat me like I'm handicapped or disabled. They just treat me like they would any doofus who fell out of his chair and sprained his butt."

While the audience chuckles, Gilda shoves Gaynor and Pierce forward.

They don't know what to do at first.

They're on TV!

Gaynor actually waves at the camera.

"You can wave at your girlfriend later, Gaynor," I say. "Right now, I need a little help."

"What were you trying to do, Jamie?" says Pierce, not too stiffly. "Audition for the part of the class turtle?"

I wiggle my arms like a tipped-over turtle to make the gag pay off while Gaynor and Pierce bend down on either side of me. They slide their hands under my back.

"Jacky Hart gave me that line," Pierce whispers in my ear.

"Thanks for the help, guys," I say out loud. "But, uh, don't you think we need to prop up my wheelchair first?"

"Oh, right," says Gaynor. "Duh."

Then he and Pierce both drop me. Hard. My head hits the "asphalt" like a rock.

I do a funny take and the audience cracks up.

Gaynor and Pierce grab my chair and roll it closer. Then, just like in real life, they lift me up and lower me into the seat.

The audience does one of those elongated "awwwws" that sitcom audiences do when they see something sweet.

"Thanks, guys," I say when I'm back in my wheelchair. "I don't know what I'd do without you two."

"Spend a lot more time on your butt," cracks Gaynor.

Ha! Now he's ad-libbing, too!

The audience howls. Gaynor sort of smiles and nods. Pierce waves.

"Who are you waving at?" I ask.

"Um, Gaynor's girlfriend?"

"Watch out, Gaynor. You might have some competition!" I waggle my eyebrows in Pierce's direction.

That gives us our exit laugh.

"Thanks, you guys," I whisper to my friends.

As we exit, Gaynor starts pumping his arm and chanting, "USA! USA!"

I'm not sure why, but the audience loves that, too!

Yes, there are no mistakes on live TV. Just new opportunities to let your friends know how awesome they are.

Chapter 62

BUYING TIME

After the schoolyard scene, we cut to another commercial break.

"Two minutes, everybody," Mr. Wetmore announces through the ceiling speakers. "And, Ms. Gold? That scene went a little long. We need to lose ninety seconds somewhere."

Gilda's nodding. Slashing her script with a thick marker. "We'll cut the cafeteria scene, go straight to the diner."

"What?" shrieks Donna. "If you do that, I'm not even in this episode."

"Huh," says Gilda, without even looking up from her script. "Funny how that worked out. Can somebody go find Bob? Make sure that our darling Donna didn't make him sick to his stomach."

"What are you implying?" Donna fumes.

"That you're off this show. Like my friend Jamie always says, being funny should be fun."

When we come out of the commercial, Nigel Bigglebottom and I do a funny scene in the diner. There's lots of yo-yoing involved. A couple of milkshake glasses get shattered.

After that, we head home to the Frownies' kitchen, where the audience discovers that Lars from Mars is my cousin.

"Let's all pose for our first Christmas card with Jamie," says Mrs. Frownie.

Stone-faced, they gather around me as Mr. Frownie sets his camera on a timer.

"Smile!" he says in the most boring monotone ever. "We're one big, happy family."

And, of course, I'm the only one even grinning. The audience cracks up.

The Frownies' cat slumps to the floor and, right on cue, puts his paws over his eyes and grumbles. Now the audience is hysterical. But the Frownies keep on frowning.

When the camera flashes, I say, "Tomorrow, we start remedial smiling lessons, you guys."

The family exits, except for Lars. He balls up his fist to threaten me. "Tomorrow," he says, "you die!"

"Great. Let me put that on my calendar."

"Was that a joke?"

"Ha!"

"Are you still trying to get the last laugh?"

"Nope. Hee-hee."

"So, how'd you even get back in your wheelchair after I decked you?" Lars snarls.

I smile. "With a little help from my friends."

We do one last scene in the diner and then go to our last commercial break.

All that's left is my closing monologue. I nail it.

The audience applauds like crazy—even *before* the applause lights come on.

"We're clear," announces Gilda, who is really getting the hang of this directing thing. "Good show, everybody."

Joe Amodio comes onto the set. "Great show, kiddos! Fantastic. Gilda, you're a natural. So, guess what I did?"

"Bought yourself an ice-cream cone to celebrate?"

"Nope. I called my alma mater, UCLA."

"Huh?"

"I went to school there. Did you enter their short-film contest?"

"Well, I was going to…"

"Forget it. You don't have to. If you can direct a live TV show for BNC, you don't have to win a contest to earn your summer internship. You're in. Plus, when you're old enough for college, the film school will give you a full scholarship. The one I'm going to fund just for you!"

"Good job, you guys," says Uncle Frankie, shaking hands with Gaynor and Pierce. "Jamie's lucky to have friends like you two."

"I've already signed a dozen autographs," reports Pierce.

"That cute girl over there kissed me," says Gaynor, pointing at Serena Wetmore. "I like being a TV star."

Mr. and Mrs. Smiley bustle out of the bleachers to join us.

"Good job, Jamie," says Mr. Smiley. "Very funny show." He's frowning, of course.

"Thanks!"

"Has anybody seen Stevie and his new friend Lars?" asks Mrs. Smiley.

"Yes, ma'am," says the lead security guard. "I'm afraid there was a slight accident. Somehow, the two of them fell into a Dumpster out back. Headfirst."

"How'd that happen?" asks Mrs. Smiley.

I shrug. "Hollywood magic, I guess."

EPILOGUE

SIGNING ON THE DOTTED LINES

The pilot is a hit.

Actually, it's a sensation. The ratings are through the roof. America can't wait for *Jamie Funnie* to become a regularly scheduled show. Neither can BNC.

And I've already called Donna Dinkle to see if she wants to be in episode two. Hey, she was a big star and then lost her show. I know how that feels, sort of. Because it almost happened to me.

Saturday morning, Joe Amodio swings by the diner with another contract that needs signing. Actually, he brings four of them—one for me and one for each of my best friends.

"You give the show a spontaneous spin," Mr. Amodio tells Gilda, quoting from our review in the *New York Times*. "'Watching *Jamie Funnie*, one has the sense that anything could happen, no matter how random or ridiculous. Young Gilda Gold has a refreshingly new feel for mainstream-TV comedy.'"

Gilda signs on to direct a dozen more episodes. "I can't do all twenty-two," she explains. "I still have homework."

"Everybody loved you two!" Mr. Amodio tells Gaynor and Pierce. "You're the best friends every kid in America wishes they had."

They sign on their dotted lines, too.

"What about that gnarly chick, Donna Dinkle?" Gaynor asks Pierce.

"She'll be back," I say. "Everybody deserves a second chance."

"I agree," says Uncle Frankie. "And, Jamie? I've always been glad you got yours."

So, what happens next?

Well, I still can't really believe it, but my best friends and I are all going to be working together on a funny TV show. Maybe Uncle Frankie's diner will become super famous. Maybe we'll all be balloons in the Macy's Thanksgiving Day Parade. Maybe Stevie will finally graduate from eighth grade.

Hey, like that review said, anything could happen.

But first, we're going to do that comedy contest for the younger kids. The ones who hang out on the elementary-school playground and try to crack each other up—just because it's fun.

I pitched the idea to Mr. Amodio. He loved it.

Gilda, Gaynor, and Pierce come with me and Mr. Amodio to see the kids in action.

Because the best laughs are always the ones you share with your best friends.

Hey, it's Jamie Grimm! Thanks for reading my story—there'll be more coming soon! But in the meantime, remember Jacky Hart? If not, reread page 180 (and maybe get your memory rebooted).

Jacky's the awesome comedian who helped me make my TV show an epic win, but she has hilarious stories of her own that you need to read! Her book is all about being a kid and finding the funny in everything, no matter who tells you that you shouldn't.

So, if you're looking for another story that'll make you laugh so hard your braces hurt, just look that-a-way. →

CHAPTER 1

Okay, let me set the scene.

It's the absolutely worst day of any year ever recorded since history has been recorded. That, of course, would be the last day of summer vacation. The day before school starts.

The year is 1990. President Bush (the first one, George *H. W.*) tells the world he doesn't like broccoli and hasn't liked it since he was a little kid, when his mother made him eat it. Donkey Kong is about as good as it gets in video games. And guys are wearing mullets. They're about as hideous as a hairstyle can be—short at the front and sides, long in the back. Kind of like a coonskin cap made out of hair.

Mullet

↓

BLINK!

I'm living with my six sisters in a tiny house near the beach in Seaside Heights. Think Little Women living on the Jersey Shore, but none of us have questionable names like Snooki or JWoww.

Our father is pretty strict. He makes sure we keep our little house spick-and-span and "shipshape," even though it's a bungalow, not a boat.

We have to do *all* of our chores before we can do anything remotely fun—even though it's the last day of summer.

"Put some elbow grease into it, girls!" That's Emma. She's only six, but she does an awesome Dad impression.

We all call Emma the Little Boss. She's incredibly stubborn but, fortunately for her, also incredibly cute.

The rest of us gab up a storm while we wash windows, beat rugs, clean up the kitchen, and scrub the toilets. Remember, this was before texting. In 1990, we actually *talked* to each other. Weird, right?

My oldest sister, Sydney, who was nineteen that year, isn't home right now because her summer ended early. She went off to college (Princeton), where she is a freshman. (Ever wonder why colleges don't have freshwomen? Are they all stale? That's the kind of goofy thing I think about sometimes.)

As you might imagine, Sydney is adored by the whole family, parents and grandparents included. She is practically perfect in every possible way.

That means she's the exact opposite of me.

CHAPTER 2

Being born a girl in the middle of a pack of girls makes me about as special as a brown M&M. I'm fourth in line to the throne, which, in our house, would be the toilet I have to scrub with stinky blue chemicals before I can go outside and have some end-of-summer fun. And with seven people sharing our single bathroom, it's no quick thing to get it clean.

I guess you could say I'm something of a tomboy. While all the other girls on the Seaside Heights beach are wearing bright red *Baywatch* one-piece swim-suits or teeny-weeny bikinis, I prefer cut-off blue

jeans and my baggiest New York Giants T-shirt. I also have a very funny sun hat. Okay, it's a sombrero.

The only sister younger than me (besides Emma, the Little Boss, of course) is Riley. She's eleven.

I feel sorry for Riley. She's in the very unfortunate position of having me as her big sister.

You see, the problem is, Riley looks up to me. She's my sidekick and partner in crime, not that we've ever done anything that's actually, you know, criminal. Okay, some of the pranks we pull are borderline illegal, but I think a halfway-decent lawyer could easily get us out of jail free (my favorite card in Monopoly). Riley is always skating on the edge of the abyss because that's where I like to hang out. In the danger zone.

You'll see.

My parents' other middle child is Hannah.

Hannah is fourteen and too nice for words. She's so sweet they won't let her into the candy stores on the boardwalk anymore because they're afraid of the competition. Also because she likes to help herself to samples of peanut butter fudge. Every day. For hours at a time.

Hannah has a huge crush on Mike Guadagno, a rich kid from Stonewall Prep. It's kind of sad and, also, kind of funny.

My sister Victoria (don't you dare call her Vickie) is fifteen going on fifty.

Victoria has advice about everything for everyone, and she *loves* to share it with you, any time of the day or night. She's a bookworm, a movie nut, and a library nerd. She also keeps a diary and likes to inform you when she intends to write about something you just did. Victoria never shuts up, not even in her sleep. One night, I'm sure I heard her giving advice to the monster in her nightmare on how to scare her better.

Finally, there's Sophia, the second oldest—or, as she likes to say, *the* oldest because Sydney is off at college.

Sophia is eighteen and in love (temporarily) with Mike Guadagno.

That's right. The same rich kid from Stonewall

Prep that Hannah has a crush on, hence the sad-funny thing I was talking about earlier. Sophia doesn't know about Hannah's feelings for Mike. Mike doesn't, either. (Victoria does and has advised against them. Repeatedly.)

Mike Guadagno is a nice guy, actually. He's what Mom would call a keeper, which means, basically, he's a fish you wouldn't toss back into the ocean after you hauled it into your boat and ripped the hook out of its mouth. I sort of feel sorry for Mike. We all do. As soon as summer's over, we know Sophia is going to rip out her hook and break Mike's heart. It's her thing. She collects boys the way a botanist collects flowers or a bugologist collects beetles.

My new friend Meredith Crawford, who recently moved to Seaside Heights from Newark, tells me there's no such thing as a bugologist when I tell her about Sophia and how she plays "impossible to get."

"Scientists who study insects are called entomologists," she says.

Meredith is super-smart. I'm hoping she'll help me do my homework when school starts. She already pitches in with the chores around our house because

she practically lives at our place and we need all the help we can get.

My mom (your grandmother) doesn't do much housekeeping. No cooking, no cleaning. Nothing.

She can't.

She's in Saudi Arabia.

CHAPTER 3

A nother thing that happened in 1990?

A crazy dictator with a bushy mustache named Saddam Hussein (the crazy guy, not the bushy mustache) invaded Kuwait because he thought they were charging too much for gas.

Hey, I don't like the price the guy on the corner charges, but do you see me invading his gas station?

Anyway, after Saddam refused to remove his troops from Kuwait, President George H. W. Bush (the guy who hates broccoli) ordered the start of Operation Desert Shield.

Mom, who everybody calls Big Sydney—not because she's large or anything but because she came before Little Sydney, my oldest sister—is a staff sergeant in the Marine Corps. The second that President Bush declared Operation Desert Shield, Mom had to pack up her gear and ship out for Saudi Arabia, where America's troops were stationed, waiting for Saddam to do the right thing, which would be to leave Kuwait without breaking anything.

MOM
with some of her pals heading off to the Persian Gulf

That's why we Hart girls are on double cleaning duty these days. We're in charge of everything in our small house, from basically raising Emma (and sometimes Riley) to checking in on Mom's mom (our grandmother Nonna) and walking Sandfleas. She's our dog.

I flush the toilet and watch the blue foamy water swirl away. My final chore is finished.

"Let's book!" I say to my friend Meredith. (Quick translation: "Let's book" in the 1990s means "Let's get outta here," not "Shall we read something by Dr. Seuss?")

"What do you want to do?" I ask, hoping she has an incredible idea that would be the perfect end to our summer vacation.

"I don't know. What do *you* want to do?"

I'm about to say "I don't know" when I have my best end-of-the-summer brainstorm *ever*.

"Let's hit the boardwalk and play a new game," I say to Meredith.

Riley asks if she can tag along.

"We might do something stupid," I warn her.

Riley shrugs. "Stupid is cool."

She'll regret that decision later, trust me.

READ MORE IN

JACKY HA-HA

AVAILABLE APRIL 2016!

James Patterson is the internationally bestselling author of the highly praised Middle School books, *Kenny Wright: Superhero*, *Homeroom Diaries*, and the I Funny, Treasure Hunters, House of Robots, Confessions, Maximum Ride, Witch & Wizard and Daniel X series. James Patterson has been the most borrowed author in UK libraries for the past eight years in a row and his books have sold more than 300 million copies worldwide, making him one of the bestselling authors of all time. He lives in Florida.

Find out more at www.jamespatterson.co.uk

Become a fan on Facebook

Chris Grabenstein is a *New York Times* bestselling author who has collaborated with James Patterson on the I Funny and Treasure Hunters series and *Daniel X: Armageddon*. He lives in New York City.

Laura Park is a cartoonist and the illustrator of the I Funny series and four books in the Middle School series. She is the author of the minicomic series *Do Not Disturb My Waking Dream*, and her work has appeared in *The Best American Comics*. She lives in Chicago.